The Vampire of

Lair of Dracula

by

Aston McAnam

Copyright © 2025 Aston McAnam

All rights reserved. The characters and events portrayed in this book are fictitious. Any similarity to real persons, living or dead, is coincidental and not intended by the author.

No part of this book may be reproduced, or stored in a retrieval system, or transmitted in any form or by any means, electronic, mechanical, photocopying, recording, or otherwise, without express written permission of the publisher. No AI TRAINING: Without in any way limiting the Authors Aston McAnam exclusive rights under copyright, any use of this publication to 'train' generate artificial intelligence (AI) technologies to generate text is expressly prohibited.

Paperback ISBN-13: 978-1-0686343-5-2
Ebook   ISBN-13: 978-1-0686343-6-9

Cover design by: Emmie Newell

Dedicated to:

To the few that believe

To the many that want to

Prologue

INSPIRED BY TRUE events in Naples, Italy, after a chance encounter.

I visited there with a good friend of mine, to see the sights of Vesuvius and Pompeii. One evening, I went for a walk, my friend chose not to as it was getting late, along the Via Vicaria Vecchia which is part of the Spaccanapoli. The atmosphere was still buzzing, and the streets were starting to become less busy. After buying a couple of drinks from a local store I decided on going back to the apartment, and it was when I stopped on the corner of Via Carbonari, where I cracked a can open and took a sip. Suddenly, a man who was taller than me, appeared and tried speaking to me in Italian. I mentioned that my Italian wasn't very good, and that is when I encountered what I now believe was the Vampire of Naples.

"Where are you from?" he asked in an accent that had a hint of another.

"I'm from England." I replied, then he said something quite strange.

"Do you know that there is a vampire here in Naples?"

I wondered if that was a question or a statement? Yet the weirdest of things was that I heard that question clearly, even over the chaoticness, as if I missed seeing his lips move. He then went on to tell me things that truly grabbed my attention, and I became partially transfixed with not only his words but also his piercing gaze. It was then that I took another sip, heard a loud bang, turned to him, and just like that he was gone. There was no way he could have passed in front of me, and when I turned to look behind in the alley...it was empty. I was bemused and astonished, for how can a person move or disappear so fast? I went back to the apartment and only mentioned this to my partner Maxine, on my return to England.

Strangely, after doing some research, we found that Bram stoker himself lived in Naples with his father during the mid-1870's, almost a decade before he finished writing his novel Dracula. Was he too visited by this tall, strangely intimidating, yet captivating man? I know this sounds crazy to suggest, but could that man be the actual vampire that approached Bram Stoker too.

Read on dear friends and make of this what you will...

The Vampire of Naples

The Abduction
Chapter 1

Present Time

THE HUMIDITY STIFFLED the air as the mosquito floated along searching for another victim. On it went as it passed a disused factory come warehouse, that promised death to any that didn't want it as the owner also required blood to function with its own wants and needs. The inside resembled the outside of some European dilapidated buildings, with sections of plaster missing or peeling off, grimy yet still strangely stylish with graffiti dotted around; one displaying the obligatory poorly drawn penis ejaculating. Windows were closed; some being boarded up with uneven planks of wood that were nailed shut. This didn't help much with the stifling heat, or the trapped stench of decay. There was a room almost reaching the ceiling on what seemed thick stilts, allowing whoever inside to spy over the now deserted factory floor, that was sparsely scattered with dusty boxes and other discarded bits of rubbish, allowing for rats to scurry in and out of. Stairs led up to the room, zigzagging a couple of times, with a step and section of handrail missing.

One of her eyes opened lazily, while the other needed a little more coaxing and effort. *'Fuck my head hurts, but another ten minutes of sleep would be nice,'* she blissfully thought in her kick-starting consciousness. Both eyelids reclosed as a strange buzzing headache drifted for a second, then splash, the harsh sensation of water hitting her face truly shocked her senses awake. One eye opened again, followed sharply by the other which had overcome the eye stick, and the usual images that we face on waking weren't recognised by her now conscious mind. Confusion caught her throat as she coughed while panic thinking, *'What? Where? What is this place?' Where am I?'* she puzzled through the fast-pulsating headache. But was it a real headache, it felt different somehow, like an intense buzzing, a sharp vibrating sensation of pain which she'd not only felt recently, but also once in her past.

Now, squinting due to a bright light being emitted from an industrial lamp shade, that swung lazily to and throw, causing more nausea and confusion as if she were on a swaying ship.

"What the fuck..." she mumbled as speech eluded escape from her lips which were stuck together with duct tape.

Not only had she woken in this strange, alarming place, with her strangled thoughts marching in time with her excruciating headache, fear also consumed her on noticing she couldn't move her arms or legs. Again, she tried to yell, but total helplessness ignited her panic as she screamed and felt a snot bubble expand then pop back onto her face, making breathing through her nose difficult as mucous danced to her erratic movements.

"What the fuck what the fuck," she tried to scream, desperately wriggling to release herself from this state of confinement but just couldn't.

Strenuously rocking in the wrought iron chair, she tried forcing herself forward and backwards, then side to side, but was caught as a fly in a spider's web, *'Why can't I get myself out of these restraints? I feel weak, what is happening to me?'* her thoughts bellowed inwardly. She was weirdly strong and beat many a man in an arm-wrestle, even knocking a man clean out with one punch when he attempted to attack her. Her party trick with college friends was to show off by getting free of any restraint, a trick she pretended was learnt whilst performing in a school play as a magician's assistant.

The tormenting light continued swaying as she noticed more of her surroundings. Sliding her eyes left and right, the captivating light only allowed for limited vision. It was then that a man suddenly appeared beside her, his head slumped chin on chest, bound and gagged as she was. *'Oh, dear Lord, what the hell is happening?'* She redirected her panic-stricken wide-eyed gaze forward, suddenly sensing someone there, as a shrill rose from deep inside of her and the petrified sound again came out muffled as the tape refused to let it break free. She continued to hear the dim toing and froing creak of the lamp, accompanied with somewhat low seductive moans, *'What the hell?'*

She could feel, no more like hear her heart pumping the blood around her body, with the rush of blood also pulsing through the veins of others that were close. Her muscles were tense, and her senses were on high alert as if she could see everything in a strange technicolour, even in this dark dimly lit room. She could make out shapes and colours that normally would not appear, and her hearing was super heightened to the point of astonishment. The man beside her was breathing slow and steadily, almost to the rhythm of a dripping pipe somewhere, and she could make out the sound of Vespa scooters whizzing up and down in the distant narrow streets. Faint voices were also heard, probably with arms flaying like sign language from the Neapolitans, but the strongest and most overpowering sense she had was scent and could actually smell the stench of fear permeating from her own body, seeping out of her pores being sickly and strangely sweet. The atmosphere within the room was cloying and bitter, but the strongest smell came from the tall imposing man in front of her, who suddenly appeared as the man next to her did. It was as if his smell was draining the strength out of her body, *'Why am I so dizzy, did this sick bastard drug me?'* She was starting to feel the panic and fear rise again, *'Oh God, I'm going to be sick, don't be sick, don't be sick, what the actual fuck is going on, I need to get out of here, and what's happened to…oh dear lord the man beside me is Brody? He's breathing but…help me Brody HELP MEEE, wake up. Jesus, he is completely out of it!'* The scent from the strange man before her was a mixture, a combination of a mesmerising musk with a strong hint of an expensive masculine aftershave. The effect was seductive, alluring and calming, yet somehow, she could sense that this could be the most dangerous man she had ever encountered.

The assumed abductor leant forward and tapped the swaying lamp with an extremely long clawlike nail, *'What the…that can't be normal?'* to give it more momentum, then he sat back. On every swing she caught the sight of his face as it appeared, then disappeared, just long enough for her to notice that he was matured, possibly in his early forties, with an aquiline nose that suited his incredibly handsome face. He had medium length hair, that was slicked back, giving the somewhat appearance of a stylish movie star, but his eyes, *'Omg his eyes,'* were blackened and devoid of life, as if you stared into nothing but emptiness. There were two figures draped by his shoulders which she shockingly realised were both naked with long dark hair falling around their faces. They were beautifully similar like twins, but one had a penis and the other without who carried full uplifted breasts as they both seductively rubbed their bodies onto his shoulders, *'They must have been making those moaning noises, that's disgusting, but…have I seen her before?'* Strangely she noticed that one had a disc like tattoo on the inside of their wrist, then realised the other had one too but close to their collarbone.

The stylish man's face reappeared, as the lamp swung back and her mind went into overdrive, for she did vaguely recognise him too. *'Where have I seen you before, where, where, where?'* His black patent shoe bobbed as he sat cross legged, and she couldn't help but notice the sharply ironed creases on his black trousers. He seemed suave with an air of aloofness, he oozed power and wealth, but she could also feel an underlying sense of danger. Unbeknown to her, the man's attempt at compulsion, that irresistible urge to make others behave in a certain way hadn't worked on her, for she was no ordinary human but something different, something extremely rare. She heard, more like sensed, a spine chilling gravelled voice that resonated in her mind. It seemed devoid of emotion yet weirdly seductive and smooth, but it didn't leave from the luscious full lips of the man in front of her.

[Hello Lillith]

She was stunned, more like perplexed, for the voice seemed to come from inside her head, a sensation she'd never felt before. How can she hear him speak when his lips hadn't moved? *'What the fuck is going on?'* she desperately thought. Then her mind shuddered weirdly, like something strange and unusual switched on in her head.

[Who is this freak?] she involuntarily propelled from her mind.

[I am not a freak Lillith; and you may address me as Drago. I maybe your worst nightmare, but not a freak, so please don't insult me with such mediocre slurs] Drago replied, again in what seemed her mind, [Now Lillith, I know you may be petrified, but I will not harm you as it is another I seek, i.e. the organ grinder]

[What the fuck, that voice, does it come from someone else in the room? His lips don't move so it must come from someone else. Wait, what, how does he know my name? No one calls me Lillith its way to formal; everybody calls me Lilly]

[It's a form of telepathy my dear Lillith, and only our kind or kind-ish can do it. I seem to have manipulated its beginnings in your mind. No doubt you will need to practice with it, but it has started for you so try and understand the low-key buzzing signal which means you are mentally transmitting. Oh, and do not swear, for I find it rather repulsive]

[Our kind-ish? What the hell does that mean? This is all madness]

She began to scream from behind the duct tape as a schoolgirl might, high pitched and annoying, whilst twisting and squirming like a deranged person.

[Please be calm Lillith and not scream like that, it's quite pathetic. For only then will I remove the tape from your mouth]

[How the fuck does he know my name? I must be going mad; the freak just spoke in what seems my head again. Seriously what the fuck is going on? Telepathy...or am I going insane? This is a nightmare, it has to be, I'll wake up soon, surely?]

[This is just not good enough dear Lillith; I have warned you about the swearing, so you've given me no choice]

"This is a nightmare, isn't it? Holy fuck I'm trapped, help me someone help me." She tried to mumble through the tape, then attempted to scream again.

He tapped the lamp once more, which gave off a soft clang that slightly echoed, but this time using a grotesque elongated finger with the same threatening long talon which ended at a very sharp point. His other hand was just as grotesque which her gaze fixated upon, as its fingers wrapped on his thigh as if the owner had run out of patience. In an instant he encompassed a container of sorts and jerked it forward causing more water to splash harshly into her face, *'Avoid the buzzing, avoid the buzzing, focus girl, that's what he said, what the hell, what the hell?'* Now she was truly shocked, and unfortunately for her this wasn't a nightmare as the lamp continued like a playground swing in a strong wind. The container slipped from the weird gnarly looking fingers and bounced itself silent on the floor killing its jarring sound. Then the man jolted forward in an instant, *'How was that movement even possible, I blinked, and he was virtually in my face.'* Then, another nano second passed, as the once handsome face he first displayed changed into a hellish sight of unimaginable terror, the sight of which hit her hard. It was a horrendous soul jarring face, truly petrifying, as the horror of it burst into view. It was wrinkly and blackened, with sunken eyes that seemed to glow red. Its jaw dropped to display sharpened jagged fangs that thrust forward as a great white sharks might when attacking, but the eyes, the eyes were penetrating and spine chilling.

"Please, please, please help me somebody anybody," she continued to muffle scream from behind the tape, while tears rolled down from her squeezed shut eyes. She wriggled in her constraints like a worm on a hook and shivered with fear like never before.

[Do I need to warn you about screaming again dear Lillith?]

She shook her head sharply from side to side, her eyelids firmly closed. *'Oh shit, the buzzing is increasing again.'*

[What is happening to me, please don't say I am in a sick kind of horror movie like Saw or Hostel?] Lilly knew she shouldn't have watched all those slasher films; the films were flashing in her mind. [What the fuck, sorry, sorry, sorry, I meant what the hell is going on, how can I get out of here?]

[Ah those horrid movies, but no, this is not a movie dear Lilith, no this is the unpleasantness of real life, where horrors upon horrors are committed on a daily basis]

He moved a disgusting hand toward her face, then ever so slowly pinched his sharp nails as tweezers on the edge of the tape that had prevented her from screaming. First, she gulped, then desperately tried to clear her throat as the tape was gently pealed from her lips, but the relief of finally getting to breath from her mouth was short and sweet, for with exhaling came the beginnings of her manic scream which was cut short as the threatening fingers replaced the tape leaving the pathetic attempt at a scream for help return to a desperate mumble.

Lilly had no idea why she and Brody were being held captive. One minute they were enjoying the sights in Pompeii, after meeting a charming local man called Giovanni who they had later arranged to meet for dinner later that evening at a local restaurant near to their hotel, and the next she was tied up and restrained to a chair. Even worse, she was face to face with this petrifying monster who seemed to relish in the fear factor. Her mind went into overdrive, racking itself trying to figure out answers, and all she could come up with was that they had been taken by a complete murderous psychopath, who was probably going to torture them one by one and eventually kill them. Danger hung menacingly in the air, and the hairs on the back of her neck were standing up as she shivered with fear, she was sure that the man in front of her could sense her terror and repugnance. Sweat trickled down her back and tickled the groove at the top of her bottom as it slid down. She desperately needed to pee, which was purely out of paralysing fear, and fiercely clenched her thighs together to stop from shamefully relieving herself in front of this monster.

Lilly slowly opened her eyes to notice Drago had changed back to his handsome self and was sitting back in his seat. He was then approached by another man who whispered something in his ear, who then turned and looked at her with a wry smile.

[Holy fuck, that…that's Giovanni? That fucking mother fucking shit, I'll fuck him up given the chance. So that's how Drago knows my real name, no one calls me Lillith. Who the fuck is Drago? Hey, now I remember him] she shuddered on recognising Drago from a few days earlier. They briefly crossed paths in the tight side streets and shoulder bumped, and that's where she felt an almost painful vibration that stopped her in her tracks, a sensation she had only sensed once before back home in the states.

[Beware your telepathy Lillith, you must distinguish between thoughts and mind talking. We can mind talk but not read thoughts. I did mention you have to work at it]

[Damn, yes, yes, give me a chance you monst…I mean Drago]

Drago cut her a stern look, then looked at the two playthings by his shoulders and seductively groped both their buttocks, followed by a dismissive wave for them to leave.

"Si, maestro." (Yes, master) they both said in unison.

He then spoke to Giovanni in Italian.

"Sei sicuro di averli controllati entrambi? Li hai scansionati accuratamente per tracciare dispositive e microchip?" (Are you certain you have checked them both? You have scanned them thoroughly for tracking devises and microchips?)

"Si, Drago." (Yes, Drago)

"Dobbiamo aspettare che l'altro si svegli, poiche la compulsion che uso sugli altri non funziona in lei. Lei e qualcosa di estremamente raro, qualcosa che ho incontrato solo una manciata di volte nell amia lunga vita, e non sono sicuro che anche lei sia stata transformata in una cacciatrice. L'operazione potrebbe richiedere del tempo, ma quando la mia sicurezza e la mia incolumita sono compromesse, adottero qualsiasi azione per eliminare tale minaccia." (We must wait for the other to wake, as the compulsion I use on others doesn't work on her. She is something extremely rare, something I have only encountered a handful of times in my long life so far. I'm not sure if she has been turned into a hunter too, therefore this might take a while. But when my security and safety are compromised, I will take any actions to eliminate the threat)

Lilly mentally tried to step out of the low-level buzzing, and back into her own thoughts, it wasn't easy *'Why is he staring at me, it's as if he's trying to look into my very soul.'*

Drago stood and began to circle around Lilly, he never took his eyes off her once, like a lion stalking its prey. Her panic and fear rose once more and, in her thoughts, she was screaming at him, *'Who are you, what do you want with us?'* Yet somehow, she sensed she needed to display the pretence of being calm and in control, however impossible that seemed to her.

[Well dear Lillith, you are safe for now, while you are here with me you are safe. I have no intention of hurting you, for you are far more valuable to me alive than dead, but…hmmm this may become problematic to me] Drago's velvety smooth tones snuck their way into her mind again. He stopped in-between his two captives, cupped his hand over Brody's head then began rapping his fingers several times. His index finger changed to be grotesque and sharp, and he scratched it along Brody's forehead drawing a line of blood that began to drip downwards. Leaning forwards, he sniffed at the fresh blood and dragged his 'back to normal' finger along, then shockingly licked it.

'Well dear Lilith, pah, he can stick his patronising tone,' she thought, dreading what may happen but strangely defiant, her eyes widened and then she closed them with a squint. *'Ok, this isn't a nightmare, it's real, it's happening. He doesn't want to hurt me, he says, right. I'll roll with this...fucking shapeshifting freak.'* Her senses started to tingle as they always have done in the past, and she began to feel strangely calmer but couldn't rationalise why, she just did.

The story of Lilly
Chapter 2

Before

LILLY HAD BEEN told her mother tragically died in childbirth which is virtually commonplace with delivering her kind. The complications of her delivery meant that her mother lost so much blood, to only then suffer a massive heart attack minutes after Lilly was born; sadly, nothing could have been done to save her. Yet despite this mournful start to her existence Lilly grew up happy having had a good and settled life with her father James, who was a modestly successful artist. He made a comfortable living for them both as they lived in the East Village, with their home filled with various pieces of art and sculptures.

So, it just remained themselves and although he had a few girlfriends over the years, not one had lived with them. Some stayed around for a while, but none became serious. When she questioned why he had never remarried, he told her that no woman would ever be able to match her mother, Adele. Lilly thought that was beautifully romantic, yet tragically sad, as she would love to see him happy and to be loved from another and not just her. There were only a few photos of her mother in the apartment, and all of them strangely shots of her being pregnant with Lilly. Adele had been a beautiful woman with long dark brown hair and eyes framed with exceptionally long eyelashes which Lilly was told she had inherited from her. The family originally came from Naples, Italy, which they had left and settled in New York during the mid-1950's. Her maternal and paternal grandparents had passed away long before Lilly was born, so it had always been just the two of them navigating their way through day-to-day life.

Lilly was quite unaware that things might be slightly different about her when she was a small girl, nothing out of the ordinary at all, just a normal little girl growing up with her dad in New York. It wasn't until she reached puberty that things started to shift and change, basically go haywire. She began having weird dreams and night terrors, an experience that petrified her and these would continue throughout her life with visions that she just couldn't explain or rationalise. Then it was subtle things that began to happen, to change in her as such, yet to anyone else it might have gone unnoticed. Like her sense of smell became heightened, as the stink from various individuals was truly sickening but unique to them. She had fantastic eyesight and at night things appeared awesome, as with a new great sense of taste and hearing, it all became incredible; let alone her strength that outstripped most in the school gym. She eventually became more introverted and stopped going as she could hear the others talk about her on the sly, cutting her jealous glances as she walked by. These unfortunately continued, and when she confronted other startled students that couldn't believe that she had heard them, she backed off and kept to herself. Things just seemed strangely normal to her as she developed with what she called her 'superpowers' which she had never been able to explain. All of her senses just felt great, and she also had an uncanny somewhat unnerving ability to sense when someone or something was near without seeing them.

The school cafeteria, a commonly noisy area, was where her hearing became so sensitive, as if she could tune into everyone's conversations. It was like watching loads of TVs at the same time, with the volume at almost full blast. At times it would become unbearable, and she would have to leave and eat somewhere quieter, she had not yet learnt how to mute certain sounds and vibrations. Then, add all the various smells and tastes which she could sense into the equation, and she would feel physically sick at times as it was just too much.

With all that was happening to Lilly, she had also developed into a beautiful girl, something she was completely unaware of to start. By the time she was 16 she had almost reached five-ten, being very slim and muscular. With glossy long dark brown hair, almost black which hung like a curtain of satin, and red almond eyes that strangely complimented her hair colour but freaked some people out. Her lips were full and lush, being blessed with flawless skin, that her father mentioned she had also inherited from her mother. It wasn't surprising with all these stunning attributes that Lilly was popular with the boys and was often asked out on dates. She would go but soon became disappointed when they turned out just to be opportunities for the boys to try it on with her. This was not what Lilly was interested in, not yet, she was only 16 and had way more important things to worry about, like her grades, and sports where she tried to fit in and not outshine the others. It confused and puzzled her on why she was different to other people, or in fact was she? Was everyone like her but just didn't talk about it?

Those thoughts were often churning around in her mind, mostly at night when for some reason she just couldn't stay asleep. When she did manage to sleep, those weird dreams continued, something that hadn't changed throughout her life with visions that she could never quite explain. They were dreams of the dead, screaming souls that had fallen from impaled bodies, necks with blood smothered on them. She had tried to put those dreams down to watching far too many horror movies, so purposely placed a block on watching anymore. But the dreams continued, as if they were visions that she had once encountered, but how?

Every night she would wake around one am and then struggle to get back to sleep. But it was at night when she created her best artwork, it was as if she had no control over her ideas and thoughts, needing to get them down on paper. These pieces would often depict scenes of darkness and sinister evil shapes, with characters that were unknown to her but strangely somehow familiar. In a way she was drawn to ghastly subject matters and really couldn't explain why, or how it repulsed yet excited her, an excitement that whirled and stimulated her mind where she constantly tried to fathom out why. At night she would sometimes speak to herself, questioning her own sanity, and wondered should she seek out a therapist to try and help her.

Unsurprisingly, it was in athletics and sport that Lilly really excelled. Her strength and stamina had developed to an extremely high standard, causing her to run faster and longer than her peers. Due to all the athletics that she took part in there wasn't an ounce of fat on her, being toned and muscular but in a feminine way. She felt free when running on the track, the wind blowing in her hair, the blood pumping throughout her body. Her muscles and joints moving rhythmically to the repetitive thud of her training shoes on the track and was powerful and strong, as was her speed in the 100 metre races. Whilst running Lilly would release questions and thoughts that were tumbling around in her mind, becoming calm and at peace with herself. By the time she was in the 11th grade at High School Lilly was in all the top teams and held the school record for the 100-metre sprint. Her hand eye coordination was excellent for the relay team, and her ability to better the long unbroken school high jump record was easy. All in all, she was one of the school's most talented athletes they had ever had.

Sadly, for Lilly all this excelling in most aspects of her school life led to some serious envy from the other girls, especially the so-called 'mean girls'. They collectively tried their utmost to make her school life as difficult as they could. This went hand in hand with the few boys she had dated, that felt spurned causing egos to take a battering and who also went out of their way to make her life difficult. Yet due to Lilly's heightened senses she could on most days outwit them, for example, when the pathetic boys put foul smelling fish liquid in her locker, she could smell it before she even reached it and came prepared to clean it out. Even when the mean girls were bitching about her amongst themselves, she could hear them, and her reflexes could thwart any obstacles they tried to put in her way at training. This all made Lilly become frustrated with her daily life as she didn't ask for any of these changes to happen to her, so tried toning everything down so that she might fit in more. She didn't want to come across as a show-off or appear too clever, or even a weirdo.

There were two events that made her crash out. The first was when cornered in the bathroom by the so-called mean girls who tried to confront her over a nothing situation. Usually, they would make sly comments, out of pure jealousy or something petty, but this time it got really heated with strong words being exchanged as Lilly had

had enough. This wasn't going to be Lilly's normal inward temper rising to the surface and her struggling to usher it away again, no this got nasty as one placed their hand on her which Lilly didn't rise to, but the other grabbed and attempted to pull her hair. With that Lilly grasped the hair-puller's neck in a choke hold and literally lifted her off the ground, leaving her legs to dangle as she pressed her against the wall. The hair-puller's gang pleaded for her to be let down as she was almost passing out and, after a moment of clarity, Lilly nonchalantly dropped her on the dirty toilet floor to the sound of her gasping for breath. It was the look of pure fear in the hair-puller's eyes that somehow satisfied Lilly, and while still shaking with rage she caught her own reflection in the mirror. She was horrified as she didn't recognise herself at all, her eyes red with rage, almost aflame, and it made Lilly want to inflict horrific pain like the night terrors that continued to haunt her. She only just managed to restrain herself from doing so, but nevertheless, it cost her a stern warning from the principal as it became a 'who was telling the truth farce'. From then on, the girls made sure to give her a wide berth.

The second was when at a party, Lilly was confronted by a jock who couldn't get over being spurned by her causing his ego to be damaged. He was drunk and with another two morons that were behaving extremely boisterously and started getting fresh with her. She asked them to stop but it became obvious to all nearby that they were harassing her, with wandering hands that grabbed at her breasts and bottom. She palm-heeled one in the chest, sending him careering into others across the room, then knocked the jock out cold with one punch. His father wanted to press charges of assault, but this was countered by a sexual harassment accusation with many witnesses to confirm Lilly only defended herself; charges were dropped, with egos further damaged.

Having a yin and yang persona, the peaceful side of her soul remained dominant, but when she felt a terrible rage creeping up inside, hand in hand with an almost irresistible urge to inflict extreme pain and suffering on the instigators, she would take herself away to somewhere quiet to calm down and reach a zen moment; to release herself from the turmoil. Those thoughts and lethal emotions truly scared her, and just before it raised its ugly head, she tried looking at her reflection in a mirror where her pallor and skin tone had subtly changed to a pale red, but not pink. This only occurred when she was almost tipped over the edge with anger, and it was unnerving to her. *'Why does this happen to me? Am I becoming possessed like the Carrie girl in the movie? How can I learn to control these intense emotions? For some strange reason I know I mustn't draw attention to myself.'*

After those two main incidents Lilly lost most of the friends that she thought she had, people had become wary and scared of her. She didn't understand what was happening within herself, and she began to worry, causing the sensitive side of her soul to pull back from others and become more of a loner. It left her feeling extremely lonely at times, where she tried to express her feelings to the very few true friends she had left, but this made her feel like a whinger. So, she ended up keeping her thoughts to herself, and even though she felt uncomfortable with them, she couldn't express or explain what or how they made her feel to others. Thankfully, Lilly and her father were close and would speak about most things, they had a 'house rule' that if anything that was bugging one another it should be discussed. They called it their 'kitchen meetings' but, when it came to talking about what was happening to herself, Lilly just didn't feel comfortable discussing such things with him.

She soon contemplated deeply on which direction to go, so decided to withdraw from her sports and concentrate on her art, for the fear of her own intense feelings and strength petrified her. Although at times the urge to inflict real pain on others was intense Lilly found that art was her solace, it truly calmed her. So, she pulled back from what some would call her 'showboating' and concentrated more on her artwork for as a child Lilly had painted, and it became her passion; it was a gift and trait she thought inherited from both her parents. She had become exuberant and excited about all aspect of art, sketching or painting all day given the chance. With the powerful development of her sight, suddenly all colours were heightened as if in technicolour, where her art teachers became so impressed with her ability to see and interpret different aspects. They encouraged her to major in art for college, having some promising scholarships and grants to help her. She eventually attended the School of Art Institute in Chicago and majored in Fine Art achieving the highest honours. Later, she moved back home with her father, who was secretly pleased as he had missed her terribly while she was away studying; the apartment just seemed empty without her there.

She was over the moon when she was offered her dream job at the Metropolitan Museum of Art on 5th Avenue. This was no mean feat as she had worked hard to get accepted and had sailed through the interview process, all the practicing and role playing with her father truly paid off.

One evening, whilst checking through her many emails, Lilly noticed an interesting one from a DNA website offering 80% off. It was strange as the company not only wanted the usual saliva sample but some blood too. This is where curiosity got the better of her, also the cheap price, so she went ahead and ordered the kit expecting it to be weeks before she received it in the mail. To her astonishment the sample kit arrived the very next day, and as Lilly nervously spat into the supplied vial, then winced as she used a small needle to collect a sample of her blood, she had absolutely no idea whatsoever what was about to unfold.

As a child she had often sat in her bedroom and romantically imagined her mother was from a poor Italian family who had travelled to America to find the American dream. Were they sculptors who had not yet been discovered, or where they famous Pizzerias who wanted to expand their successful family business? She was eager to find out who she had inherited her dark looks from, as her dad was a typical white American, blond, blue eyed and tall of Swedish descent. She was keen to discover if she had any living relatives still in Naples, maybe some cousins or elderly aunts and uncles. For some reason she couldn't fathom why, it was a calling as such, and she didn't mention to her father what she had done. Although they talked about her mother frequently, she felt this was quite a personal thing to do and didn't want to upset him by probing and delving too deep into her heritage.

When the email came through a couple of weeks later, Lilly was excited and slightly nervous to open it. Her finger hovered over the button for a few seconds, then she thought *'What's the worst that can happen.'* But, in that instant, her whole world exploded catastrophically. Lilly couldn't understand or believe what she was reading, it couldn't be right, the company must have made a mistake. It was there on the screen, right in front of her, stating that her father, the man she had always believed and had no reason to think otherwise was in fact not her biological father. He was in no way related to her, with the obvious fifty percent Italian, and the other strains from Eastern Europe? *'What the fuck does this mean, dad hasn't got any family there.'* Lilly thought to herself. Her mind went into complete overdrive, *'if he isn't my father, then who is? Who the hell is my real dad, is he alive, where does he live, do I look like him?'* All those questions rushed through her mind, and when her father returned home that night, Lilly was waiting for him by the door.

To say it was a difficult evening for them both was a major understatement, but Lilly attempted to stay calm and let her dad explain what she thought couldn't possibly be true. Her father had to be honest and truthful by opening old wounds and secrets that he had hoped would have been shared while Adele was beside him, but sadly that wasn't the case. He revealed to Lilly that he wasn't her natural father, and that when he met her mother she was in the early stages of her pregnancy.

Her mother never revealed who the father was, it was a quick holiday romance that she had in Naples whilst she was discovering her family roots. She didn't know much about the man, not even his full name, and she didn't know she was with child on arriving back home in the States. When James (her father) met Adele, they instantly fell in love and when she discovered she was expecting she was honest with James and told him he wasn't the father. James decided to stay with Adele as he didn't care and chose to believe that Lilly was biologically his.

That evening was a heavily charged night of emotions for Lilly and James, which drew tears from them both, but the father daughter love they dearly had for each other was strong as they hugged while she said.

"You will always be my father."

***

A week later Lilly was at work in her favourite part of the Museum, the Archives. It is her calm place, somewhere she can leave her worries at the door. She was tasked in restoring the most beautiful of rare paintings, and while it was painstaking work she was in heaven. She often pinched herself in the morning on having landed such an interesting and lifelong dream job and didn't even mind that her colleagues were mainly older men; with the aroma of mothballs and mints permeating the air. She was too engrossed in her work, and the sheer beauty she was witnessing each day. To balance that off she got to mix with some of the younger members of staff when she went for lunch in the staff cafeteria.

One Monday lunchtime Lilly was in the queue to get her usual serving of Mac and Cheese, a favourite of hers because it was delicious, and even better than her dad's, when she spotted a new kitchen server. He was tall, with blond hair struggling to escape from its net cap and had the cutest dreamy blue eyes she had ever seen, with eyelashes that out-beautied her own. But it was his smile that caught Lilly's breath, his teeth were perfect, and his lips were just asking to be kissed. Lilly felt herself blushing and almost lost the ability to speak when she caught his eye.

"Would you like any salad with your serving ma'am?" he asked.

"Err yes please, th-thanks," was all Lilly could respond.

"Hi, I'm Brody, it's my first day here, and you have just made it brighter for me. Is it too forward to ask your name?"

"It's Lilly, I thought I'd never seen you before. How's it going so far? Are you enjoying it?'

Lilly was trying to delve into her head and find something interesting to keep the conversation going but could see that the queue was growing behind her, she just didn't want to stop looking at him. He was unbelievably cute.

"It's going well funnily enough," he replied with a quick wink, "but it sure has just got so much better."

Lilly took her tray of food and found a table where she could sneak a cheeky peak at the man, she now knew was called Brody. Strangely her appetite had disappeared, and she was all flustered. She could sense that he was grabbing quick glances over at her too, and then there he was, standing in front of her.

"Have you finished with your lunch Lilly? Can I take your tray for you, and well, can I ask if you would like to meet me for a coffee later? If that's not too presumptuous of me?"

Lilly did a mental fist pump and attempted to act cool replying.

"That would be lovely Brody, and no its not presumptuous of you. I would love to go for a coffee. I finish work at 6, is that ok for you?"

"Cool, shall I wait for you on the steps by the main entrance later?" Brody's blue eyes were twinkling at her with interest.

"That'd be perfect, I'll see you later, I must get back to the basement now hee-hee," she giggled, "but I'll see you soon, thanks." *'Thanks? Why did I say thanks? That was like when people say, 'see you later' and not only have you just met them, but you'll never really see them again?'* She walked off towards the exit and couldn't resist taking a backward glance to see if Brody was looking at her... he was, *'yes.'* She went back to work with a spring in her step and just knew she would be clock watching until 6. She had been on a couple of dates whilst at college, and a few since she'd left. But sadly, due to her senses she could sniff out timewasters fairly quickly, with most of the dates not getting past a third one as the 'ick' factor often took over. She didn't feel anything was off with Brody, as her Spidey senses hadn't started tingling yet, but she had only just clapped eyes on him so tonight would be the test.

The coffee date went kind of well, and so far, Lilly didn't get any ick feelings from Brody; except the topic of conversations were rather limited. He was the perfect gentleman that evening, walking curb side to the coffee shop, (a sign her dad had taught her about manners) to him holding the door open for her and even pulling her chair out and not sitting down until she did. Lilly loved old school manners and Brody was ticking all the boxes so far. He was attentive but not too nosey with the conversation flowing naturally, and by the end of the evening she had agreed to another date for later in the week. They swapped numbers and he said he would call her in the morning, then made sure she got a cab safely. She looked out the rear window to see him waving at her.

Soon Lilly found herself and Brody falling into a good friendship of sorts, it all happened quite fast yet steadily. Lilly loved that Brody didn't expect anything sexually from her, he was happy to take things in that department slowly and not to rush, *'Could he be any more perfect.'* The only thing that Lilly was curious about was how Brody funded all the dates that he took Lilly on, as he refused to let her pay for anything when they went out. He lived in a nice neighbourhood and his apartment was furnished well. When she questioned him about it, he would evade answering and divert the conversation. *'Give him time, he will tell me when he is ready',* she thought, *'maybe he had inherited money and doesn't want to talk about it. Or did he have to do some kind of community service order?'* Something didn't add up, and Lilly just couldn't quite put her finger on it, and although she was unaware of his true identity or purpose; her senses started tingling slightly. Things seem to be just too perfect; she wanted to believe that he was genuine, *'yet how does someone who works in a museum cafeteria afford to live where he does? Still, I'm a big girl now and can handle myself if he got silly.'* So, she went along with it.

One evening, on a date in an Italian restaurant, that Brody orchestrated, he finally mentioned that he came into a small inheritance and just wanted to enjoy himself for once. Brody then guided the conversation towards a trip to Naples, possibly visiting Vesuvius and Pompei and to explore the galleries and museums as he knew full well Lilly adored Italian artwork. She was blown away with his thoughtfulness and more so his generosity of paying for it all, so quite naturally jumped at the chance. So, she requested some time off for a vacation and told her Head of Department that she was travelling to Naples to sightsee. Her boss was very excited for her, and recommended they visit the Museo Capella Sansevero and the Museo Archeololgico Nazionale, as they hold some stunning pieces of art.

Before the abduction

Lilly instantly fell in love with everything about Naples, the smells, the sounds, and the vibe of the city. In some strange way it sensed like she had come home, and she just couldn't explain it, she felt complete there. Was it because her maternal grandparents were from there, who knows?

Whilst Lilly and Brody were exploring on their first evening, after eating at a restaurant called the Pizzeria Brande, said to be the place where the Margherita pizza was first invented, they devoured a delicious pizza and insalata caprese, They eventually found themselves in the narrow dark side streets trying to find their way back to their hotel which was the Grand Hotel Oriente, it was off the tight, chaotic side streets of the infamous Spanish Quarter. As the streets became narrower and darker Lilly began to get the 'ick' feeling with Brody as he became uncharacteristically cowardly and most definitely not the gentleman, she had taken him for. The fact that he was clinging on to her like a limpet made her want to puke, '*what a wimp*' she thought to herself.

They walked past a couple of men in the busy Spaccanopli, with its straight and narrow main street that traverses the old historic centre, she had to be aware of where she was walking as the scooters were whizzing past her and people were strolling in all directions, when she ever-so-lightly brushed against the taller of two men and they both took a backward glance at each other which caused Lilly to virtually stop in her tracks. She was instantly overcome with a chill that ran like a shock wave through her body, and began to tremble with an unexplained fear as a cold sweat also came across her at the same time. She caught the man's eye, sensing something nefarious. Brody seeing her face, asked if everything was ok, as she looked petrified. Lilly began to feel strange, even unwell, as her head began to bang like an orchestra bass drum being hit rapidly. It was accompanied by a vibration that was piercing yet amazing and almost grabbed and lifted her with ecstasy. Her head continued to whirl as the tall man's gaze seemed to burn into her as he turned to say something to the shorter man. Then, in a blink of an eye, he was gone, with the other man just walking along by himself.

"What? Where did that tall man go?" Lilly demanded in a stunned tone.

"What tall man Lilly? Are you ok?" quizzed Brody.

"The man that was staring at me, that man over there was walking alongside him."

"Yeah, sure, that's right, a man did look at you, kind of scarily, but I just thought he was checking you out. I mean, you're a great looking babe. I don't know what happened to him, I looked away and he was gone. I can only see the back of that other man over there now. Are you sure you're ok Lilly?"

She felt extremely peculiar, like her inner self wanting to leave but her body held it prisoner. This internal turbulence caused added mayhem to her now estranged thoughts making her want to get back to the hotel as quick as possible and laydown. After they arrived at the entrance Brody made up some nonsense about wanting to go for a walk, so Lilly huffed and went to the rooms on her own as he obviously couldn't be bothered to be with her. That was the first thing she didn't like about him, well that and him not being the sharpest tool in the shed which made conversations dull and slightly boring. He even openly displayed impatience and ignorance when she attempted to sketch something and then behaved like an adolescence when he spotted the huge penis of the fertility god Priapus at La Casa dei Vetti, on a poster advertising Pompeii tours. He giggled like a young teenager which really annoyed her displaying no appreciation of classic art, and now he displayed selfishness to add to the newly formed 'ick' list. *'Sometimes a man needs more than good looks.'* she mused.

Present time

Now, however, back in the derelict warehouse, she glanced over at Brody and noticed he was slowly starting to come round.

The charlatan Brody

Chapter 3

Before

ESSENTIALLY, BRODY HAD been referred to as a prize piece of shit, albeit a very handsome and charming one, but still a piece of shit who has strolled through life using his stunning looks to manipulate everything to his advantage. Learning from a very young age that he had a certain effect on women, and occasionally men, that he could use fully to further himself. He wasn't very intelligent, he didn't go to college after High School as he wasn't smart enough, but he had learnt impeccable manners from his grandfather which the 'older' women mostly loved.

Realising jobs in bars and clubs were a great place to meet women, he received money and gifts from them while he perfected his art by charming them into bed after a few drinks; being a smooth talker, a pathological liar, and what some would call a true bullshitter. So, with his smooth talk which was basically the same drivel that he had read in romance books he had plagiarised, he became very popular with older ladies who seemed to have an endless supply of money to burn. He was often 'paid' for his company, a form of gigolo, and duped women with stories such as 'I've a hundred-thousand-dollar check waiting to clear but my father's boiler has broken and I'm short of five thousand to fix it.' It was a scam like many others, as he was a serial scammer, and it worked brilliantly. He literally had no morals, not even a sniff of empathy for who he would hurt or more often than not destroy along the way. All he cared about was receiving money to continue enjoying his lifestyle, then and only then was he satisfied.

So, he discreetly advertised his services and was sometimes paid to be a honey trap for rich businessmen who had suspicions that their so-called 'loyal' wives were up to no good. It developed into quite a lucrative hustle for him and the perks of the job were a bonus.

It was through this side of things that Brody caught the attention of a certain businessman from Argentina, who had contacted him a few years earlier. Apparently, he was some kind of hunter called Carlos, and quite how he managed to hear about him he didn't know or particularly care, even though the assignments sounded crazy. In fact, when he first heard what it was for, he did a double take, as he was to lure a vampiress who liked good looking men. At the time Brody thought this was a joke and assumed it was for a porn film, which he didn't normally do, but the payment was going to be more than most, so he agreed. It was set up and fastidiously planned by Carlos, but just before the so called vampiress took the bait, something went wrong and an innocent woman was killed in the crossfire which actually meant nothing to Carlos, his heart was as black as the thing he hunted; it was just collateral damage to him, as what he hunted slipped the net and he was furious.

This bothered Brody, not so much about the poor innocent woman who had lost her life, but on how serious and obsessive he was about the so-called hunt. He'd met Carlos several times since, but only once at his rented apartment which was truly weird. It was like something out of a detective movie with a massive board and pictures, that strangely had slightly blurred faces, A4 notices, even post it notes scribbled with all kinds of stuff, with pinned strings going from one section to another. It was crazy, like a messed-up spider's web, but hey, what did Brody care, he got paid so whatever.

He eventually became a freelancer for Carlos, and over the next few years was used as a snare to trap those that were involved in illegal business dealings which is how Carlos made his money, for his supposed 'vampire hunts' cost money. Brody had a natural ability to adapt to any situation, whether it be setting up cheating business partners for blackmail, or Carlos' unhealthy obsession on catching said vampires. It all just seemed to be a mere fantasy that he had, so Brody went along with it and humoured him. He got paid; he didn't care; it was easy money for him.

All things changed the day Carlos offered him a job which had an expense account, an apartment in a nice upmarket area which was furnished, and a whole new wardrobe of clothes. This totally suited Brody for he was shallow and vain, a total narcissist. The only thing that slightly ruffled his feathers was that the job he had to take on was to work in a canteen at the Metropolitan Museum of Art. Brody hated the smell of the kitchen, all the greasy smells clung to his hair and skin, for he was a hugely conceited man feeling this was way beneath him, and could only see two advantages for this current assignment. One being the huge amount of money he was getting, and the second meeting Lilly, who he had to admit was the most stunningly beautiful young woman he had encountered.

While studying her file, that had been given to him by Carlos, he found himself being transfixed by the girl in the photos and believed this was going to be the most pleasurable assignment to date. In fact, it was the best kind of honeytrap, and the bonus of luring the inexperienced Lilly to Naples was the icing on the cake. He had to create the illusion of a genuine persona to win her over, so went for the mysterious rich young man who had inherited a small fortune yet still wanted to work for a living and not let his wealth take away who he was; quite pathetic but he ran with it. He decided to keep this 'story' from Lilly for a while and let her wonder how he managed to sustain his lifestyle on a meagre wage from the Museum, for in his head this would all add to the illusion that he was a decent man. Brody knew he would find it a struggle not to seduce Lilly from the get-go, but he was under strict instructions to take it slow and behave in a gentlemanly manor, 'Ha, act gentlemanly, what a joke, I'm the complete opposite in every way.'

So, he did as he was instructed, taking her out for coffee dates to start with then progressing onto dinner dates and picnics in Central Park, always behaving perfectly with good old-fashioned charm and manners. He quickly became bored with the fact that she seemed to find herself funny, and to be so passionate about her job, something he had encountered many times in the past, and always found dull. When women expressed feelings such as those his thoughts often drifted towards a beach in the Bahamas as his usual shallowness and vanity often replaced their interests as he truly didn't care. He had to firmly remind himself that this was just another assignment, a very fruitful one, and when it was over he would take himself off to there or Mexico to sun and charm his way through more holiday 'romances'. He was also sternly instructed to keep an eye on Lilly and not to let her out of his sight when they arrived there, and mostly to be aware of anyone who approaches them both. 'Make sure the burner phone I gave you is always with you and always charged. Do not let Lilly see it, do you understand?' Carlos demanded.

***

Everything was going well in Naples until Lilly supposedly saw a man and then suddenly felt strangely ill, she almost collapsed. Brody helped her back to the hotel then left her alone in their room, something he was specifically told not to do, using this opportunity to phone Carlos to let him know of what had just happened and how it spooked and unnerved him, but he didn't pick up. So, Brody impatiently waited, pacing up and down in the lobby on a six step turn around, then received a text message saying:

CALL WHEN SAFE TO DO SO.

"Carlos! Look what the hell is going on? Lilly has got me all spooked."

"Are you with her?"

"Of course not, I'm on the phone to you, you told me to keep the phone from her."

"You fool; I clearly told you to be with her at all times."

"Don't get your panties in a bunch, she's secure up in the room, and I'm in the hotel lobby so calm yourself."

"Nevertheless, get back to her pronto. Did you take her to the areas I told you to?" asked Carlos, he couldn't help with his excitement.

"What? Yes, and then she became ill."

"Who did you see?"

"Well, there was this man, I looked away for a second, and in a flash, he was gone."

"Oh my God, it's easier than I thought it would be. Ha, this is brilliant just brilliant. This is as easy as when they found Richard the thirds grave."

"What the fuck are you on about Carlos?"

"Never mind. I didn't mention this to you before, but it's who I'm after. Ha, it's what I've hunted in the past, but unfortunately, that didn't work out too well, but I was right he's still there."

"What the hell? Don't tell me this is another of your pathetic vampire hunts? They don't exist. I thought this was just another business hustle or honeytrap?

"Well, it's not. You didn't ask so I didn't tell."

"Well then, what the bloody hell is it?"

"Lilly is there as bait."

"Bait? Bait for what? What the hell is going on Carlos." Brody nervously waited but no reply came, "I said ba-it for wh-at?" he tried to repeat sternly but became croaky.

"A vampire, an extremely dangerous one."

Brody went quiet and began to ponder. Firstly, he presumed it was one of Carlos' fantasy vampire hunts, but it was the way Lilly reacted to the man which fazed him. The whole situation was truly alarming.

"Look Carlos, I was just playing around with your imaginary friends, your wild goose chase so to say. None of your others were real. Vampires are a myth, a made-up story, because nothing happened before on any of your 'hunts' and nothing will happen now either. It's a load rubbish...isn't it?" a gulp got stuck in his throat this time.

"Brody you fool, they are real, they are just extremely difficult to trap. Now I know for a fact that this one is still there, I must get the ball rolling, because last time I lost a few m... I mean I almost lost my whole ear."

Brody continued to argue, he just found it hard to believe vampires were real, and became even more disturbed with what may happen, becoming even more fearful. Carlos reminded him about his job and to wait for the outcome to be paid, but Brody was beginning not to want any part of this, it wasn't what he signed up for.

"Lilly is the key in Naples, just don't ask me why." snapped Carlos.

"What key? What the fuck is going on?"

"Listen you moron, I have paid your expenses, now finish the job if you want to get paid the rest."

"You fucking douche bag, I thought this was an easy job, the usual honey trap. How dangerous is this going to be? Tell me you piece of shit or I walk. Am I in any danger, because if you don't tell me the deal is off, I'll cut my loses." Brody almost chocked on yet another gulp.

He tried to call Carlos' bluff, but the stress of not getting paid made him sweat even more so.

"Then you won't get paid, and you don't need to know all the details. All you need to know now is that she is the bait. Now stop whining and get on with it, do you want your money or not? Or shall I inform the police of the little hustles that you do, they would be very interested."

"Don't threaten me!"

"I'll give you an extra ten thousand dollars a day, on top of what we've already agreed, but only until this is all done."

Brody went silent, he was stunned and couldn't believe that kind of money but pushed for more.

"That sounds like danger money, this is dangerous, isn't it?" Brody's voice sounded worried, then Carlos hit him with a huge dangling carrot.

"You'll get a substantial bonus of one million dollars if we catch him, ok. Ten thousand today and the rest will be on going, on a daily basis."

"Holy fuck Carlos, it's a deal. I'll check my bank account and if it's not there…"

"It has already been deposited, but one more thing, beware of its underlings. They will approach you soon I expect. So, remember what to do, it's most important!"

"Yes, yeah, I'll do what you told me to do."

"Don't forget, with wealth comes risk, just remember that. If we don't catch it then you'll not get your bonus. Just know that the element of surprise is paramount to us. Past vampires have slipped the net, and it'll not happen again, got it. Now get back to her, fast."

The call ended with Brody being told more information, that truly unnerved him, but then again, he just put it down to Carlos being a raving lunatic and shook off his anxiety. So, he'll tread carefully as he thought of the money, the carrot was just there ready to be grabbed.

***

The next day, even though Lilly was slightly off with him, they took the train to Pompeii, and as already mentioned what might happen, they were approached by a charming Italian called Giovanni who was accompanied by his girlfriend. Lilly absolutely loved their wit and banter, so when Giovanni suggested dinner later that evening Brody was highly suspicious but went nervously along with it and agreed. This was starting to freak him out as doubts on him getting the job done weighed heavily on his mind, for fooling a person was one thing, but putting himself in possible harm's way was another. Nonetheless, the money was mind boggling to him, and even though it dampened his worries he was still stunned when Carlos told him at the end of their conversation who the vampire potentially was. What Carlos was seeking wasn't the most powerful vampire, but the most famous. So, considering the pathway to all that cash, Brody hesitantly continued with the masquerade and thought of nothing but the money.

Later, after they met Giovanni, all Brody remembered was going for dinner, then being tied up and in hell.

The torture of a liar
Chapter 4

AFTER HIS BLACKOUT, Brody began to stir.

[Ahh, are you finally awake?]

Drago telepathically thrust those words into his mind which Brody found stimulating, even invigorating, almost calming him, but then he quickly became aware of being tied up and restrained to what he presumed was a chair, thus panic commenced.

"W-w-where did that voice come from? Where the f-fuck am I?" he mumbled from behind the duct tape that was securely stuck across his mouth.

He attempted to force open his sticky eyes which finally sprung wide to reveal a lampshade toing and froing, and that's where he caught sight of a face that fleetingly appeared before him. It drifted out of the shadows then disappeared back into darkness, to only reappear again as the face now loomed towards him and only stopped a few inches from his nose. Brody couldn't tear his eyes away from the image and shrank into his chair, his head almost sideways as he flinched, for it was the face of the man that Lilly had bumped into the previous night, possibly the same man that Carlos warned him about.

"Holy shit," Brody softly mumbled, the words barely leaving his lips, "it must be him, I'm well and truly f..." his head lowered slightly, indicating he was talking to himself and at a loss, but, in truth, money was his incentive, so on recalling his conversation with Carlos he began to hum…very loudly.

'Why the hell is he humming like a madman?' thought Lilly.

"Ahh, humming…really," said Drago, "trying to block me out, are you? Who told you about that nonsense?"

Brody glanced sideways and spotted Lilly then desperately began pleading for help, with his widened eyes and pulled to eyebrows, while pathetically trying to wriggle free. Knowing he was in deep shit; he frantically thought of how to get himself out of this nightmare, and of course to save his own skin.

"Are you looking to cause me harm?" Drago asked.

Brody shook his head manically from side to side, unable to be heard due to the tape that almost prevented him from breathing, but his humming continued.

"Why don't you tell Lillith who you truly are Brody, I take it that is your real name?" the voice that previously came from inside Brody's head was now coming from the shadows, its seductive tone continued, "or is it another name, as you own multiple passports, don't you? So, which one is it today? You see I have found out some very interesting things about you, and let's be honest you are extremely stupid, or how is it the British put it so well…a sandwich short of a picnic. Why don't you start by explaining what was in your bag. You see I had Giovanni; you remember him, don't you? Well, he dug around and checked you out. By the way he found what must be a burner phone, with only one contact number on it, very strange don't you think? So, whoever you are, why have you come to Naples with Lillith?" Drago palm heeled his own head as if surprised, "oh, how foolish of me, I'd better remove that tape otherwise how would you answer," Drago leant forward and ever so gently peeled the tape away from Brody's mouth, "there, now you can answer."

"Who the fuck are you, what do you want with me, I don't know anything" Brody screamed.

"Please don't attempt to insult my intelligence you imbecile of a man. I will ask you again, why are you here in Naples with Lillith? Also, why in that particular section of the city? I have done extensive research on you Brody and it's made for quite an interesting read; shall we divulge to Lillith your sordid little lies?"

Drago barely had time to peel the tape from Lilly's mouth, when she screamed.

"What the fuck is going on Brody? What the hell have you done? Why are we here? Tell me you son of a bitch before I fucking explode," she yelled, "this is all wrong, what have you fucking done?"

"Listen Lilly, don't be angry…"

"Don't be angry? Look at us, LOOK AT US?" she shouted at him.

"Now, now children, don't let youth get you by the throat." commented Drago.

"I don't understand," she continued, "are you in partnership with Drago?"

"Drago, who the hell is Drago?" Brody quizzed with a quivering voice.

Lilly continued to rant, but Drago interrupted her with a…

"Shhhhhhh, Lillith, please be calm, for I have information to extract from the beautiful Brody, who may not be so attractive after I've finished with him," the seed of what was to come was planted, "how did you possibly manage to afford traveling to Naples first class Brody? To stay in such an opulent hotel on your meagre salary working in a kitchen, and the clothes you are wearing, they would surely suit someone from a far socially higher standing than you?" The insults hurled at Brody were meant to chip away at his superficial confidence and inflated ego, it was working.

"Tell him of the money you inherited." insisted Lilly.

"Ha," said Drago, "he's a complete charlatan, and has lured you here on false pretences. Now Brody, who were the calls to? Who are you working for?"

Drago now reached over with long grotesque fingers, which truly startled Brody, and grasped his head in a vice like grip. Holding it firmly, the pressure built-up in Brody's head, with his eyes feeling as if they were literally going to pop-out. Fear and pain overtook the quivering con artist as he involuntarily wet himself. Knowing he couldn't reveal anything he just moaned in agony, because he'd lose that massive bonus, yes, the bonus that would set him up for life. Therefore, he decided to take the pain and hoped it might be all worth it.

"There are consequences when you play with the Devil beautiful Brody," Drago turned and looked at Lilly, "would you like to know more about this so-called man? You see Brody, Lillith and I have become slightly more acquainted whilst you have been unconscious, and it's been quite enlightening for her."

"There's nothing more to know about me Lilly," Brody mumbled, lying to win her over to his side, "he's mad, a liar, don't listen to him, he's…" but before he could finish Drago stooped down and shoved a short length of rope between his teeth for him to bite down on, then securely slapped the tape back across his mouth.

"Oh, the joy of heading off your words of deceit at the pass," Drago glared at Brody, "prepare for pain…"

The whites of Drago's eyes turned red, his stare seemed to burn into Brody's own, and his face became the horrifying shape that terrified Lilly earlier. Fear stifled the air and without an ounce of empathy, Drago grabbed Brody's hand then placed a talon just under the tip of his index fingernail.

"Holy shit," Brody's unintelligible voice muffled, his eyes almost bulging out of his head as he tried to screech, "what the f-f-fuck are you? Is it all true? Was Carlos telling the truth? What are you doing? Don't you fucking dare, don't you fuaaaaaargh…"

Drago slowly pushed his talon under Brody's fingernail, it lifted from the skin, and the sound of excruciating agony continued to screech from behind the tape. Brody's toes involuntarily strained upwards as the pain short circuited his senses, while blood seeped from the fresh wound; and unfortunately for him, this was just the beginning of his torment. Drago did the same thing again to another nail then leaned over to Brody's left ear, and never once breaking eye contact repeated the question.

"Why are you here? Who are you working for?"

Lilly was paralysed with fear and found it hard to speak, totally filled with horror. Even when she turned away from the grisly sight, she could hear the desperate strangled screams.

"P-please stop." she managed to ask, the words more of a whisper.

Drago paused from beginning on yet another nail and looked at her.

"Stop it, stop it, just stop it, why are you doing this to him? He's obviously trying to tell you something, so remove his tape for Christ's sake."

"You're absolutely right in your assessment dear Lillith," said Drago, to the sound of desperate breathing, whimpering and crying coming from Brody, "but it does beg the question, will he still persist in not revealing his true reasons for being here with you?" he turned and looked at Brody, "do you want me to carry on torturing you, as I must admit I do find it exhilarating. You see dear Lillith, I must drive the point home, ha yet another pun?" Drago drawled.

The torture continued in a slow, methodical, yet evil sadistic way. Drago's aim was to inflict as much pain on the spineless weasel of a man, so he started on Brody's thumb. He had misled and lied to Lilly, in fact their whole relationship had been a lie, and was only in it for the hefty pay packet. Brody really had no emotions when it came down to deceiving others, even though Lilly was stunningly attractive, money was his only true love and at the end of the day he was out for number one. He was unable to answer, gagging and chomping on the rope secured by the suffocating tape, and would have divulged anything at this point, absolutely anything, but he was trapped in a nightmarish terror as the inflictor of pain wanted to prolong his agony and suffering, for it suited Drago. Brody's body violently trembled as the unrelenting pain sizzled along his fingertips, and when it finally became too overwhelming, he succumbed to the pain by passing out which was a relief to Lilly's ears.

"Why are you doing this to him? Give him a chance to answer." a deeply disturbed Lilly questioned.

"I'm surprised you have asked that asinine question once again Lillith. Why, you ask me? Why? Because I enjoy it that's why. I'm enjoying it dear girl, but ok, just one more thing to do before I stop as the following will be extremely painful to him. But please understand, I will inflict whatever for the information I need."

Brody was slumped forward, chin on chest, saliva drooling from his mouth, but he was soon awakened with a bucket of water forcefully splashed into his face from Giovanni, after a nod from Drago. He came round with the look of 'shit this isn't a nightmare; it's all truly happening' on his face, with his hair hanging down as the water competed with his sweat, he shivered with a combination of fear and agony.

"I need the truth from you Brody. You are a very vain man aren't you, and you would hate to lose your looks, yes! But let's be honest that's all you have going for you. As I have already mentioned, there isn't much going on upstairs is there, you're not intelligent at all are you."

Brody could hear the voice coming from all around him, as if he were being circled. Drago stood back to admire his torturous work and pondered on what to inflict next. Tapping his chin with an elongated fingernail, he quickly placed it against Brody's forehead and began to drag it. Then with his other hand he held onto his head firmly and scratched the word 'Liar' across his forehead. Blood dripped from the splitting skin, causing Brody to squeeze his eyes shut while the warm sticky fluid trickled down forming thin red streaks. Moving his sharp index talon along Brody's nose and lips that were still taped up, Drago began slowly gliding it as if he were planning to painfully slice them off.

"In my past, when I lived the life of another, I was partial to cutting off ears, noses, but that was then. You are a useless piece of humanity beautiful Brody, I will let you rest for now, but I am not finished with you quite yet, I need to speak to Lillith."

Drago turned his attention towards Lilly, with her extremely pale skin, as he had suspicions about her from the beginning. He had Giovanni quickly do a background check on her and if true, he would have to keep her safe…for now.

"Dear Lillith, I require you to tell me of your parentage, your history, who are, or were, your parents?"

"Why do you want to know about them? What's it to you? If you're after a ransom you can think again, I have no money. Brody has more than me." she hissed back at Drago.

"Just answer my questions Lillith and you will be saved from any pain, unlike your friend here. He is going to suffer so much, aren't you," he patted Brody's cheek, "you may choose to watch or not, the choice is yours, after what you hear you might just be inclined to watch and enjoy."

"Ok, ok, I'll tell you if you don't hurt him anymore," Lilly complained as Drago raised an eyebrow, "my father is called James. I live with him in New York, he is an artist."

"And what about your mother Lillith, tell me about your mother."

"I never knew my mum; she died giving birth to me. Why do you want to know about her?"

Drago leant forward after sitting back down in his chair, his interest was piqued and his dark eyes flashed. Lilly felt a sudden sharp buzzing in her head.

[Keep going Lillith, I need to know more about your mother, tell me more] Drago's voice filled her mind.

"Her name was Adele, her family was from Naples, she was an artist like my dad. Before I was born, she went back Naples to find out more about her heritage. According to my dad she had a holiday romance with someone and when she got back to New York she was pregnant. The rest you know, she died."

Drago kept firing questions at Lilly, what did she look like, how old was she, where did she stay in Naples and so forth, until Lilly's emotions became too much.

"Enough now, just stop, why the interest in my mother, don't tell me you knew her," the colour then drained from Lilly's face, her heart rate increased, and she started hyperventilating, "please no, no, no, you did know her, didn't you?"

Drago's eyes flashed, his body tense, a piece of the jigsaw had fallen into place. He turned and told her.

"Lillith, I know exactly who you are, and why you are here. You are being used as bait, for this excuse of a man, who has used you to get to me. That's all I will reveal for now," he glared at Brody, "I require you to inform Lilly of your true insignificant self. Now, I will give you one more chance before I start to lose my patience with you."

Drago ripped off the duct tape and Brody instantly spat out the mangled rope followed by an ear-piercing howl of pain, in between attempting to get as much air into his lungs as possible, breathing like a woman about to give birth; short sharp quick breaths to try and suppress the pain. He then struggled unsuccessfully, and pathetically truth be told, to get free from his restraints while he looked over at Lilly for help. She in turn stared at him with a combination of horror and utter bewilderment, somehow his pain thrilled her inner being.

"Please, please, stop," Brody whimpered, "ok, ok, I'll tell you…please…can I have some water; I need some water." he pleaded, swaying side to side, his sweat and dribble rolling onto his chest.

"Dagli un po' d'aqua." (Give him some water) Drago ordered Giovanni.

Brody leant forward while Giovanni angled the cup allowing him to gulp it down.

"Well?" Drago said displaying an air of impatience.

"Carlos is his name!"

"Carlos? Hmmm, tell me, what does this Carlos look like?" he continued to question.

"He…he spoke with a Spanish accent, you know heavy with that throat clearing lisp sound, and funnily enough he looked Spanish, you know, dark hair but with light skin," Brody waffled, as he looked at the state of his swollen fingertips, "oh, and he's missing the top part of his left ear, which he tries to cover with his hair, he just reminded me of a mad professor gone madder. He's the one who's paid me for this job, expenses and all. I was just told to get to know Lilly and bring her here to Naples, that's all I know, I swear."

"Well riddle me that," Drago said softly, "yes, I have met him before, once in the past to be exact, quiet an interesting man. You see it's not the cowardly, for there are many, but the determined few that are dangerous. I place him in the category of the latter."

"Hey, look man, like I've already said, he calls himself Carlos, aargh the pain, the fucking pain aargh, I've only ever met him once." Brody replied lying, he didn't want to reveal too much information as the fear of losing out on all that money amazingly topped the pain that had been inflicted on him.

"You are making a mistake in choosing not to answer my questions truthfully Brody. Met him only once you say? Do you truly enjoy pain? I will allow you a few moments to think carefully about your limited options." warned Drago as Lilly took over the conversation.

"Why did you lie to me Brody, I trusted you. Was it all just a lie?" Lilly moaned at him, almost heartbroken.

"Look, all I know is that I had to bring you to a particular area, go out in the evening until it was very late, that's all I know."

"But why would you do this Brody, why? Was it for money?"

"Look, it wasn't personal, but of course it was, it's always about the money honey. You were just another job, a very well-paid job, and now it's gone tits up for me," he replied with more bravado than he felt, "and you, you sick bastard, let me go and I'll give you the address of the man who paid me for this job, he is the one you want, not me…ha…and he wants to kill you so badly. Let me go and I'll tell you anything you want to know."

With a swift action Drago placed the tape back over his mouth, slapping it down, then fiercely flicked his talon slicing the tip of Brody's right ear with a single swipe. It's barely attached skin allowed it to dangle, with blood seeping out as Lilly watched transfixed. At that point Drago leant forward and seductively licked the flowing blood, while all Brody could do was watch as Drago lowered his hand, then raised it again and with his extremely sharp talon began sawing at the rest of his ear;

it finally bounced off Brody's knee then plopped onto the floor. Even with the duct tape Brody's muffled scream was loud and riddled with desperation.

Lilly couldn't move, even if she could have, she was frozen and transfixed with the torture Drago was inflicting on Brody. She felt a mixture of pure fear, disgust and anger at what was being done to him, yet there was a conflicting side to her that was so enraged at Brody for all the lies and deceit put to her.

Drago fleetingly revealed his true self as he lowered his face to Brody's neck, his teeth baring their razor-edged fangs, then sank them into his flesh with a thud and started to feed; only sucking enough blood to satisfy his need, a snack as such. Lilly found herself transfixed with Drago's bite, almost wanting to snuggle up beside him and watch closely. It was then that Brody humiliated himself by losing control of his bowls, the pain was excruciating for him, so the smell of blood and shit filled the air. He was stunned by what had happened to him, mainly the bite, and went into shock, tensing up then passing out through raw pain again. Drago flung his head back, with blood dripping from his fangs into the air.

"Do you really think that I will let you out of here alive you poor disillusioned soul," Drago said to the unconscious Brody, "you are now my bait, and Lillith should surely see your true cowardly colours, don't you think? He has put you in a very dangerous position Lillith, and sadly you will not come out of this alive regarding Carlos, unless I help you."

Lilly was terrified on witnessing the horror inflicted, yet she was somewhat drawn and partially excited, almost aroused at the sight of the blood which Drago fed on. Deep within her she knew this was wrong, yet she couldn't control what she was feeling, *'Oh dear Lord is he a warped madman, or truly a vampire, but I want to taste his blood too and watch his pain. Wait, what the fuck is wrong with me? Stop it Lilly, get a grip.'* she thought while her mind whirled almost out of control.

Drago ripped the tape off Brody's mouth, after noticing he had thrown up, with the sick spilling out of his nostrils, it looked disgusting like the man himself. He ordered Giovanni to clean him up and to bandage the seeping earhole, then Drago left the room. It was a while before Brody came round, whimpering from the throbbing pain of the torture which had been inflicted on him.

"Help me Lilly, aargh, please help me. He's going to kill me don't you see, aargh the pain the pain aargh, the fucking cunt cut my ear off," Brody was quivering in fear, his voice almost a squeak, then he lost it and yelled out with an insane scream, "HELP ME, SOMEBODY HELP ME, PLEASE."

"Nobody is coming Brody, and how the hell can I help you? Look at me, I'm tied up too. I've a feeling he doesn't want me any harm. Just tell him anything he asks, and Drago might change his mind."

"Well bully for you aargh, that he might not cause you any harm, look what he's done to me, he's ruined me, and who the fuck is Drago? Why do you keep saying that name?"

"What? Are you truly an idiot Brody. The man that did those horrible things to you, he's Drago."

"Holy shit, is that what it told you? He's true name isn't Drago you fool; he was Vlad the Impaler."

"W-w-what the hell are you on about? Have you lost your mind? That's impossible."

"What am I on about you ask aargh, don't you fucking get it, aargh, it hurts so fucking much," he sucked air in as a hiss, the pain was almost unbearable, "Vlad became a supposed vampire, well that's what Carlos told me and I know it's not a fantasy anymore, aargh the pain the pain, stop this fucking pain aargh…" he moaned sweat pouring from his tortured brow, "that sadistic bastard you call Drago is fucking Dracula."

"What the…"

"Yes, fucking Dracula himself."

The becoming of Drago/Dracula
Chapter 5

How he came to be.

LILLY'S THOUGHTS WERE marching in time with her thumping headache, *'No, no, no, my father is human and can't be a monster, a vampire, especially the most famous. This is a nightmare, a dream that I must wake from.'* [This must be a nightmare, I've got to wake up, he just can't be my father] she calmly let loose with newly discovered telepathic thoughts.

"This is not a nightmare, nor dream, dear Lillith...sorry to sound like a scene out of that movie Star Wars but, I am your father." answered Drago as he seemed to appear out of thin air on re-entering the room.

"No, I don't believe you, it's just a coincidence, I am not half monster, I just can't be, no, no, no I can't be, I just can't be."

[Only you can decide on that Lillith, I have nothing to gain by lying to you as that imbecile has done]

Brody sat slumped; the exhaustion of pain sent him into a semi-sleep.

"Have you ever questioned your lineage or history Lillith? Are you not curious to know who you truly are?" Drago asked, a slightly taunting look spread across his sinister face, "shall I enlighten you on your true parentage or shall I keep you in torturous ignorance?"

"Go fuck yourself you freak" Lilly spat at him.

"Now, now, Lillith, that's not a very ladylike way to speak, is it?"

"What the fuck are you on about, there is no way on this earth you are my father. My mother would never have gone anywhere near you, you are a monster, how the hell did this happen? You must have this all mixed up; your mind is full of crap." Lilly was shaking with a combination of fear and rage which shook through her body, the restraints were tugging against her as she struggled to get free.

"I'm deeply surprised with your reaction," Drago replied with irritation creeping into his voice.

Lilly's mind raced over the DNA results informing her that James wasn't her biological father, it flashed in her thoughts. Surely this couldn't be true, there had to be a mistake, this evil monster in front of her, taunting her with these vile lies couldn't be her father, could he? Her mother wouldn't have slept with him unless she was drugged or even worse raped, all these thoughts were running through her mind. He must have coerced her into having a relationship as no one in their right mind would have done so willingly. Drago began explaining to Lilly how he met her mother and the briefness of their relationship, informing Lilly of her history and heritage.

"Adele was a beautiful young woman when I came across her here in Naples. If I remember correctly, she was here exploring and investigating her Neapolitan heritage. One evening whilst I was out walking, rather hunting for another, I saw her dining alone; her head was down engrossed in a book. She had luscious long dark hair swept around one shoulder exposing a smooth beautiful neck that was calling out to be caressed and kissed, I immediately felt drawn to her vulnerability and beauty. There have only been a few times in my long life that I have felt anything akin to feelings, for as a vampire I rarely have emotions. We travel through this eternal life without the connections your type seems to require and yearn for. But on rare occasions our past human lives slip through. Meeting your mother was one of those rare moments, our attraction to each other was instantaneous, and I fought hard against the desirable urge to feed on her blood. It was an internal battle with my wanting to change her into a vampire, to keep her forever, it was truly overwhelming."

"Oh please," Lilly rolled her eyes sarcastically, "you wanted to 'change' her, really, you expect me to believe this fucking bullshit? What is this, something from a movie?"

Drago glared at her with frustration, his eyes flashing red in anger, as Lilly didn't care about being polite anymore.

"Lillith, I have requested several times for you to stop with the profanities. If you will just care to listen, I will describe to you, my conundrum. It is a common myth that vampires are easy to create, and only the uneducated think they can be made at will. Believe me we are rare, but not as rare as one such as you. We are extremely fussy with our choices, because if we get it wrong it would lead us to getting bit in the backside, if you pardon the pun. You see, a newbie vampire may expose us through their bloodlust or even turn on us, so it's not a case of making the right choice, the problem is what we might create. Only the right kind of human can be converted, as it's rare for a human to accept our blood as most will perish during conversion, it's an excruciatingly painful death to experience or even watch. When we die to be reborn, not many survive the transition, otherwise the world would be awash with vampires. But there was a problem, a very dangerous problem that I had to address," they glared at each other, his stare slightly more intense than hers, "now, before you so rudely interrupted, let me get back to when I met your mother. A short while later I introduced myself to her and we got to know each other over a late dinner. We would meet in the evenings and spoke all night in between making love to each other. Adele was truly an innocent soul and eager to learn the art of lovemaking, she was a willing pupil."

"Shut up, just stop talking, I don't want to know any more of this bullshit. That's disgusting I don't need to know about you and my mother having made out, or did you get into her mind? Did you rape her you fucking animal?" Lilly screamed at Drago; her eyes were blazing with anger, she took a deep breath, calmed, then quizzed, "wait, just…can you go back a bit, you said something about hunting?"

Drago continued, as if Lilly wasn't there, he seemed to have transported himself back in time reminiscing over a past love.

"I battled everyday with my yearnings, and I made the decision to cut all contact with Adele. She was an anomaly for me as I hadn't felt those yearnings, those feelings and emotions which was akin to love for many a long year. I knew that every time I was with her, I was putting her in danger of her life. We can be described as becoming worshipful towards our lovers' skin, becoming obsessed with them, and I was truly obsessed like another was. So, I cut her off from my existence, I never knew what had happened to her, even if she had returned to America or not, and I certainly had no knowledge of your birth. I can see by your expression that you assume this to be just confected nonsense dear Lillith, but this is the truth. Wait, are you…are you doing an attitude roll neck?"

Lilly said nothing and instead just glanced at the pitiful Brody beside her. He was mumbling as if delirious, his body a mess from the handsome man she had fallen for. She looked back at Drago which he took as a cue to waffle on, *'Even Vampires have egos'* she thought, then asked.

"You've avoided my previous question. Were you hunting her then?"

"Ahh yes, about the hunt you ask. There was a frenzy created by a killer vampire many years gone, that lured other vampires here, but there can only be one and I am that one. You see we stalk each other for dominance, but it is I that have always been victorious. Yet, there was a presence lately, before you were born, that had unnerved me, a presence that felt so powerful I feared that I may lose. Another anomaly had arrived from the new world, your world, a blood traveller as we call them, and not self-locked to a specific place as most vampires have now become. One that stalked by a woman's side, to keep her to himself. You see she was a descendent of the sister of his great love, a love he longed return to him. She had the same look, smell, and it longed for her touch again, but it knew in its obsessed way your mother wasn't she. Unfortunately, it had tried to convert its past lover so it could be with her forever, but her veins boiled with its vampire blood, then she was no more. That descendent was your mother and in its confused desire, its scrambled mind was fogged, so I took advantage in killing it after a ferocious fight. It took me a couple of days to truly recover, but then, like it had done in the past and as absurd as it may seem, I fell desperately in love with your mother," Drago paused, as if he were again deep in reminiscing, then asked, "have you ever wondered why you have more strength than your peers Lillith, why you can sense things that others seem not too. Do you ever feel a rage inside you so strong that you struggle to contain it. The rage of pain that you have inherited from me, the desire of seeking blood from others, the desire to inflict pain and destruction on others. Do you feel it Lillith, coursing through your veins. Are there times that you fight to control the demons deep within you. At night do you dream of horrors so real that others couldn't possibly comprehend or begin to understand? They are hereditary thoughts, it's called epigenetic transgenerational inheritance, totally subconscious experiences that seem like a déjà vu. There is no proof it seems so the jury's out, but then again…how does a cuckoo know it's a cuckoo. This is your heritage, Lillith; you are my child."

"That's just madness; I don't deserve any of this. I'm a good person, well I deeply try to be, and now I'm prisoner to a…a…a vampire, who's calling me his daughter? Madness, utter madness."

"I hear they call your kind a Dhampir, Pah, how pathetic a word you humans use, you are merely half breeds, or mix breeds to us, be you mainly by accident and as I've already mentioned extremely rare."

"So, now you're saying I was an accident?"

"Maybe I should have worded things more differently, more like an unexpected happening. Forgive me, English is not my first language."

"An 'unexpected happening' sounds awful."

"The funniest thing is, you are actually classed as a mythical creature dear Lillith, even more mythical than me. You see, dhampirs do not need to consume blood, so can eat and drink. But you may need to consume blood as a healing method through your bloodthirst, it will help as you are vulnerable to severe wounds and will help you recover fast, just remember that. You've already noticed you can detect vampires and its visa-versa, even when they are in disguise, and once you have mastered your senses you can scramble a vampire's mind leaving them open to hunters. You see the weaker of us can become obsessed with dhampirs, and therefore make terrible mistakes, that's why Carlos or his ilk have used you, for they use humans to do their dirty footwork first. Somehow, he has figured that you exist, that man is so obsessive, he's truly incredible. I am fully aware of the vampire hunter Carlos who found out about my true existence a decade past and wants nothing but to destroy me. He failed miserably after our first encounter, and I would imagine he wants me dead even more so, wanting to totally remove my linage for the sheer prestige of it all; that's why you are in danger. Now, I gather he tries again to calm his damaged ego, to lure me out, and now knowing I'm no push over as the last time he will come at me hard. His arrogance nearly cost him his life, well it cost the lives of his accomplices. He has wanted this for so long, and he must feel like this is his chance by using you as bait. Dear Lillith, you are so extremely rare, and let the truth be known I was never aware of you as a child, but it all makes sense knowing that your dear mother died whilst giving birth to you."

Lilly was filled with exhaustion, she had enough of the shear madness which overwhelmed her, it was as if a fuse blew in her head and all she could muster up to say was…

"Oh, why don't you all just fuck off, fuck off the lot of you bastards. You don't know me, you don't have the right to tell me who I am or how I feel, or what my thoughts may be. Just fuck off and leave me alone. I don't know what you want from me." she began to cry, the tears making tracks down along her cheeks.

Drago pointed a long-elongated finger at Brody who was slumped unconscious, still drooling with long strings from his mouth attaching to his chest.

"You thought you were going on a romantic vacation to Naples, but sadly no, you have been used as bait by this erroneous human. Lillith, you have been used to lure me out for the hunter to hunt, and now I must turn the hunt onto the hunter as once I am dead, then surely you will be too. So, in a nutshell, I am saving your life dear Lillith. You know, I instantly sensed you were nearby the other day, as you turned the corner I felt you, I could sense the vibrations coming off you were strong. That's what I whispered to Giovanni that night, so he dug around and used one of my many contacts to trace all incoming visitors arriving here in Naples, and you were highlighted to me. Do you really think it was a coincidence that you met Giovanni? You naïve woman, it was all set up. Giovanni bribed the consigliere at your hotel and accessed your room. The idiot beside you didn't do a very good job of concealing his burner phone, it was so easy to access it."

"Please leave me be," Lilly exhaustedly replied, "just leave me be, my head is going to explode. How can I digest or take in anything you are telling me, and I have no desire or intention of watching you doing whatever you are going to do to him," gesturing with a nod towards Brody, "or this so-called Carlos."

She was completely drained emotionally and physically, never had she felt so petrified, pitiful, confused and angry at the same time. Her instinct was to fight her way out of this nightmare and the urge to kill this monster in front of her was overwhelming. She felt herself vibrating with rage the blood coursing through her veins, and her head pounding painfully. Lowering her head she breathed in and out deeply, the humidity suffocating the air, then closed her eyes as exhaustion overwhelmed her.

***

Lilly heard voices, ever so softly at first which quickly got louder as she began blinking to the rhythm of her pounding headache. Her eyes opened to the realisation of remembering what had happened, the living nightmare continued as the voices turned into Italian words being exchanged between Drago and Giovanni. Annoyingly the sound of Brody moaning and drooling through his nose continued. *'I just want to go home to my dad'* she mournfully thought.

"Ahh, Lillith, you are rested yes," said Drago in his usual sultry voice.

He whispered something to Giovanni who instantly grabbed a plastic water bottle and splashed it over her head, then placed the rim on her bottom lip. Lilly gulped it down with enthusiasm, the stuffiness of the closed off room had dehydrated her to point of dizziness.

"How long have I been out?"

"Not too long my dear," Drago purred, "but it gave us time to prepare."

"Prepare for what?"

Drago simply looked at Brody, insinuating Carlos and his accomplices will be arriving soon.

"I have a powerful presence here in Naples, including a network of underlings, worshippers, devotees or even groupies if you like, in fact, you will never guess who they are; they are below me and know their place. Some look at me as a demi-god, it's that I seemingly have a Svengali appeal. Our bites are which entice them you see, it captivates and seduces; it comes with a shot of a chemical that triggers feelings of intense pleasure causing a flood of dopamine that hit's their senses. From then on, they will be hooked and will need more. While others work for me and I use them to my benefit, paying them handsomely for their discretion. Many are high up influential contacts, lawyers, judges, government officials, even the police, and they will do anything I ask of them. We vampires are not being chased by an angry mob baring pitchforks and lit torches anymore; times have moved on dear Lillith, and we have become savvy. Like when I sensed you, I used my contacts at passport control to find your identity and orchestrated Giovanni to make 'accidental' contact with you both whilst you were sightseeing. Yes, my underlings will do anything asked of them, at any given moment; my influence goes far and beyond the norm. Why, even as we speak, I have people checking flight logs for certain names or for anything out of the ordinary that might prove useful. Some are even watching and guarding the outer perimeter at this precise moment, but believe me Lillith our killers are coming, if not are here already."

Lilly became fascinated, and wanted to understand who this Drago was, it became mentally motivating. There was no way of escape, so her thoughts started dancing around with questions. If he were the legendary 'Dracula' then why was Giovanni and the others calling him master, and at times Drago?

"So, dad," she smirked, "who are you? Drago or Dracula?" she followed with one of those 'mwahahahahahaa' supposedly evil laughs, but in essence it was just a sarcastic sound.

"Are you truly aware of who I am?" his self-centred side shone through.

"You've insinuated that we have to wait for this so-called Carlos and his gang," they peered at each other, "so please, enlighten me. Everything I've ever heard or watched about vampires is third hand, so, let it be from the horse's mouth so to say."

"I was born, I lived, I died to then be reborn as the so called undead. What more do you need to know?"

At this point Lilly wasn't sure if she would make a break for it if her hands and feet were untied. *'Maybe he's right, maybe this shit Brody has sealed my fate, maybe being with this…this thing…might keep me alive, but I still want to at least try and be untied. I'll play along with Mister Mwahahaha,'* she mentally manoeuvred.

"No, that's not enough. That's nowhere near enough. I want to know about you."

He stared at her and, whether she wanted to hear the truth or not, Drago proceeded to tell Lilly about his long, murderous, yet eventful life. His voice was constantly smooth and seductive, and she found herself reluctantly becoming captivated with his tale.

"Life has always been exciting through my existence dear Lillith, but the centuries have become so much more exhilarating. Now we have cars, technology, with more money and things readily available. Dracula is a name I used many centuries ago, it has now become defunct, as Drago is the name I use now. Dracula is far too menacing, don't you think."

"So, you think you are… or were Dracula?"

"Hmmm, there is an undertone of derision in your question. Let me tell you my story," he waved Giovanni away, then settled crossed leg in his chair, his sleek hair and sharp stylish clothing added to the maestro about to conduct his story. The swaying lamp had long since stilled itself, so he tapped it, probably for affect, allowing it to swing once more as he continued, "I haven't told my story to anyone for many a year, but seeing you are who you are, you should know. I was born to the name of Vlad Tepes, in the 15th century. I was a Prince, and later to become a rather brutal warlord. I must admit the stories are very true regarding my cruelty which included torturing, yes that which I used on him and the impaling of my enemies onto stakes, which I can still do to you if I wish," there came a squeal from Brody, "it was a method of execution and to instil fear into my enemies, mainly for the Ottomans."

"Wait…what? You are actually saying you were, or are, Vlad the Impaler? You are joking me…"

"Do not interrupt dear Lillith, let me tell you of your heritage. I was the son of Vlad Dracul ruler of Wallachia and was supposedly born around the 1430's," he did that palm down tilting side to side gesture to indicate roughly, "no one truly knows the exact date, in a place called Sighisoara. When the Ottomans finally ambushed me and my troops, I was supposedly killed late 1470's," he did that hand movement again, "I was apparently decapitated, and my head sent to the sultan in Constantinople. I was roughly in my forties on my human death."

"What? That's it? Not enough, I need more details."

"More?" he smirked, "ok, you see, one of my patrols reported a strange happening to some of the impaled bodies," Drago continued, "holes were spotted on some of the victims' necks, and those bodies being an awful shade of grey as if drained of blood. You must understand dear Lillith, superstitions were writhe long ago, and stories of blood suckers soon spread, Upirs as they were first called, and that news could paralyse an army through fear."

"But how did Vlad become Dracula?"

"Yes, that is a story to tell. I was not the original vampire, but I later became the most famous. Mainly because of Bram and strangely it was all down to one of my bodyguard's who killed that original vampire, if that was what it truly was, and in so doing unintentionally created me. You see we stalked this thing one night which was draining blood from the dying impaled victims, and during the battle to kill it, it converted me."

"That's it, really? There must be more to it than that?" she quizzed as Drago sighed, then furthered his story.

"It was a battle within a battle and while the Ottomans set upon my vastly outnumbered troops, they had no idea that some of us were already pre-engaged in a ferocious fight against a vampire. Thunder shook the surroundings accompanied by torrential rain making things difficult to see, as lightning flashed and lite up the vampire before them. Its hideous face displayed protruding fangs dripping with blood causing those close to recoil in horror. Thunder boomed again followed by a deafening crack, that rumbled as the next bolt of lightning revealed the vampire to be gone. The screams of men soon became apparent with limbs being torn off and hurled splattering the warriors with blood, including the backs of those that fled in utter terror. The vampire leapt from one staked decomposing body to another, faster than a spear could reach it, and on every leap, it swung its grotesque hand decapitating the unfortunate below it. As both sides of the battle intensified, the roar of the Ottoman attack caused confusion, and I was heavily struck by the vampire sending me hurtling into a rotting stake that snapped in half. The force knocked the wind out of me, I could barely breath, as the vampire was bearing down for the kill. So fast in fact I barely had time to swing my sword at its arm that narrowly missed my throat, but its fangs were on target, and they buried into my neck. The sheer shock and violence were countered by intense pleasure as it exsanguinated my body of blood and astonishingly, in that brief moment, I reached what some would describe as sheer extasy. It made no sense, and when it pulled back sharply, it displayed a horrific glee in its eyes while raising its head as a wolf might howl, ready for the death bite. In truth I was saved from death by a severely injured bodyguard who somehow managed to muster up the strength and swung his sword that sliced through its arrogant neck decapitating it. The headless torso was incredibly heavy as it crashed down trapping me and I virtually drowned in blood, for it poured from its neck into my mouth, choking me, almost drowning me in its burning gore as I unavoidably drank in my future dark fate. I endured this for what seemed an eternity, then what appeared to be death overtook me, as the passing of the original vampire accidentally gave rise to a new one. You see, it wasn't treachery that killed me, for it had been rumoured that I was assassinated by my own men, but my human life was taken by all things, a vampire. Vlad the Impaler was to be no more, and the rise of Dracula had begun. You see, the old vampire was a powerful one and those traits were to be mine now; I had become a damnation of God as it were. The now victorious Ottomans, curse them, mistook the vampires head, which was exceptionally similar to mine, as the wounded bodyguard that did the decapitation misled them from the truth, and it was that head which was presented to the sultan Mehmed the second in Constantinople. The fools delivered the original vampire's head as mine, ha!"

"So, it wasn't Vlad, I mean you, that was beheaded."

"Obviously not, no, that story was a total misconception, it was the original vampire itself. Again, my loyal bodyguard fooled the Ottomans by having placed my body into a coffin, for he didn't want me to be buried in a mass grave with the other corpses."

"Holy shit, what a fuck up! You, the famous so called 'Dracula' was literally an accidental vampire. Oh, dear

Lord what a twist of fate. The sheer irony of it all, what a f…"

But before she could utter another word, he sprung forward with lightning speed and she received a stinging slap.

"Daughter or not, I have warned you specifically and repeatedly about profanities."

"You fff…" her cheek felt like it had been punched, as she breathed in deeply then expelled while gritting her teeth tightly, while petulant infuriation welled within her and she wanted to blast foul curses at him, but wisely chose not to, reeling her neck in was the best way to go, "I mean you…you monster."

"Yes, and don't forget it…so, furthermore to the story," he gave her a soul jarring stare, the kind a killer would give before killing and she shuddered, not through fear but her blossoming defiance, he continued, "the Turks who were still stationed there became paranoid and with great haste dispatched my coffin to my daughter in Italy where they received a pittance of a ransom, for the beginnings of scratching sounds came from the inside of the coffin which were terrifying to hear. Slow spine-chilling nail drags scraped along the inside, the beginning of my transition. 'He must be alive' they said to each other, but none were brave enough to look and see. Yet, the exact circumstances of my death have been spun and spun, eventually becoming unclear to most. One theory was that monks found my torso in a forest clearing and carried it into a crypt, another that I was taken prisoner, but as already mentioned my supposed dead body was ransomed to my daughter in Italy to then be buried. I must say, it is strange with circumstances, for just before arriving here there was a violent storm which covered my tracks over people going missing on the vessel, that was after I had to unfortunately suck my way through the rats of course, and that dear Lillith is how eventually I arrived here in glorious Naples."

The tattooist
Chapter 6

"HAVE YOU EVER been here before?" an incensed but still inquisitive Lilly asked with a slightly swollen left cheek.

"Yes, I had visited Naples on occasion in the past, and my daughter Maria had a crypt built in the church of Santa Maria la Nova. You know, just by the main alter, there is a floor crypt, and there you will find the fat face of a vampire I allowed to live, one of the few. Somehow, archaeologists were sniffing around and seem to have put two and two together, noting different artists have a different take on what they see and create. The truth is artists never quite achieve similar expectations, hence why dragons and faces become dissimilar. Therefore, after their damn research, and unfortunately for me, some even say they have evidence that confirms the tomb of Vlad i.e. my past life, is here rather than in the monastery over on Snagov island. Some animal bones were stuffed into that one, and now the emphasis has shifted to Italy."

"What about other places? I mean, where else have you travelled?"

"I have travelled the world, managing to hide in plain sight so to speak; but I returned and settled here in Naples. You see dear Lillith, at the time I was never the only vampire here, there were many with battles of hierarchy going on, and as I have already mentioned we are extremely territorial. These confrontations, more like squabbles which had been going on for centuries prior to my arrival are truly pathetic. You see it's all about the feeding rights, no different to animals that protect their patch, but these often resulted in playground fights. When I came back here, for obvious reasons, and became the main vampire through extreme violence I must say, not allowing any other vampires to settle here from then on. In fact, I became the only vampire in the Neapolitan region, no, the only one south of Rome. The other is in Venice, a complete snake and backstabber that has returned from the south of the Americas, and I will kill her one day. But, as for the others, we have reached a truce of sorts, agreeing not to encroach on each other's territory, and on the rare occasion we have used each other to gather information when it has deemed necessary. For there is a network of us vampires across the world, as we have moved into the modern world of trade and business. But some are more unscrupulous than others, those I avoid."

"Wow, that all sounds crazy, I mean truly, but it does seem like you've taken to this place."

"Yes, much has happened here. But one of my best moments, most captivating moments, is when Giuseppe Sanmartino created the Veiled Christ and homed it in the nave of the Capella Sansevero in the mid 1750's. A magnificent marble sculpture in its purest form, and is truly a sight to behold, with its delicate intricate beauty. He led me to the balcony before and above where it lay, both his hands covering my eyes for the surprise factor. I was actually excited for I knew of his great craftmanship, and when he revealed the beauty of it, I gasped, for what a sight to behold. I leapt, no floated down to get a closer look at this vision of beauty, to touch and glide my fingers along it, desperately needing to caress its glory. My whole being danced within, the emotions of utter joy became excruciating, and my sheer amazement collided with ecstasy. I ran my fingers along the pristine marble and only just refrained from throwing myself over it as intense emotions prickled my skin with a rush that jolted me. I actually cried blood, something I have not done for many a year, with a drop leaving my left cheek to fall and splash onto the statue's beautiful lips causing me to cry even more so. I held and caressed Giuseppe for a very long time, for it was and still is magnificent."

"What…wait, you knew the artist? You knew Giuseppe? Oh my God," she felt as if her skull was held in a vice, the tension built and she needed to get her jumbled thoughts into some kind of order before her mind exploded, "dear Lord…I…I'm just astonished by all of this. Yes, it seems you are what you are, but…but you truly are a walking echo from the past of sorts, for someone with my interests this is just way too overpowering, it's truly amazing." she almost whispered those last few words.

"Much have I seen in my life dear Lillith, but I can assure you there is nothing as stunning as the 'Veiled Christ'."

Lilly found herself reluctantly warming to Drago, whilst listening to his appreciation of the arts. How can a monster that is responsible for the killing of countless thousands, show such depth of artistic understanding. Surely someone so evil must have shreds of humanity left to describe how he felt when he came across such splendour. The description of his eyes bleeding through tears of joy over the pure beauty of it all truly moved her. He stared at her, then shifted gear.

"I have lived here amongst the population of Naples with ease for centuries as they have never bothered me, for I have only taken what I need. Nevertheless, I must say, I do have a particular penchant for their blood, it has a rather intoxicating flavour. It was also here that I changed my name to Drago, as I have already mentioned, it's much less menacing of a name. Lillith dear, us vampires are not the habitual monsters of old as the movies portray, time has moved on and so have the others like me across the globe. We don't creep around in the shadows anymore, that isn't what we do, and I no longer skulk into the catacombs of Naples, we have had to move with the times and adjust."

"But the movies and countless books written about your lot, are any of them true? I mean…are any of the myths true?"

"Contrary to the litany of myths and counter myths, most are mere tales and exactly that…myths. Confected stories that show a fixation on utter movie rubbish, yet then again, I suppose it sells. Conversions are extremely dangerous, and creating a new vampire can be creating your own enemy, no matter who it once was. It is too much of a risk because there is a strong chance that they can be overcome with bloodlust and give the game away by going into a killing frenzy with irresistible urges that are uncontrollable to the inexperienced. But, understand this dear Lillith, we remain mostly loners and refrain from proliferation, because as mentioned the game is up if we get it wrong. Saying 'get yee gone' to the crazed mob doesn't work anymore as most would flee, but there has always been that handful of persistent annoyance who would push their agenda and hunt you down. The hunter would then become the hunted."

"So, you're telling me it's all rubbish, you know, what's said about you lot?"

"What I'm telling you is not the fuzzy side of vampires; this is the reality of being a vampire. It's an understandable mistake people make, that we can be changed back; this is not a temporary change, it's permanent. You see dear Lillith, it takes time for the transformation to happen, a couple or a few days and does not come about instantly or overnight, regardless of what has been said. At first, our bodies seem dead to the uneducated, so are buried alive, no more like buried undead, and that is where they remain until they shrivel up and truly die if they do not feed. So, perish they do, if unable to release themselves, but the few that survive become vampires after escaping their potential doom and the horrendously painful adjustment to their DNA breakdown, causing a rebirth, therefore we are literally reborn a vampire; don't ask, just accept. The cremated ones are obviously gone instantly."

"Is that why the Turks thought you were dead at first?"

"Yes, but as my transformation began, they heard the slow scratchings from within the coffin and basically crapped themselves, taking buttons for the ransom of my body after my daughter heard of my death."

"You were lucky, I mean, being in a coffin?"

"Yes, that can be said, but the incredible odds against me becoming who I have become are astonishing, yet here I am. It may seem I show a careless lack of care, are heartlessness yada yada yada but after all, I am Dracula," he gave a slight nose in the air superior smirk, "I must say, I still find it truly astonishing how this vampire noir remains foremost in the minds of the many, its cliché being the Bram Stoker novel which totally highjacked the vampire theme. You see, Bram's notion that good defeats evil is, pah," Drago blustered in contempt, "in fact evil is truly inherent and cannot be addressed, he failed to comprehend my words."

"Wait! What do you mean, 'he failed to comprehend my words'. Are you saying you met him?"

"Why yes dear Lillith, I met him here in Naples, late-ish 1870's if I remember correctly. He was on a street corner waiting for his father."

"Wow, that's incredible, I mean you meeting him," she paused, "oh dear Lord, did he get his inspiration by meeting you?"

"Some may make the assumption that he did, if they only knew."

"That's amazing, but surely, he was right about good defeating evil, that's why you…err…die."

"Utter nonsense, he rushed the ending as you can clearly see by looking at me," he gave a theatrical bow, "he fell in line with Victorian beliefs and values. You see, evil may skip one maybe two or more generations but eventually it will return, even in what seems the most perfect family linage. Evil always conquers all, where religion only does its utmost to suppress it, but unfortunately, there is no escape. For even evil must be used to defeat what seems evil, temporarily of course. Evil always comes up on top, therefore always wins."

"So poignant, I mean your words and thoughts, but what is true?" she paused, "I mean, what are your superpowers, ha." she half laughed.

"We can only shapeshift from what we were, to what we have become, it took some practice but once mastered it's easily done, hence my hands and appearance. Oh, and the fangs thing, our teeth move forward as a great white shark does for the bite attack. I can become taller or shorter, thinner or fatter in a virtual heartbeat and I can inter fix my human looks with the vampires, as you have noticed with my hands and face. Shapeshifting to look human or vampire can be compared to…example being the mimic octopus that can change its shape, colour, texture and behaviour to mimic other sea creatures; it's the best comparison. Being superfast and having Herculean strength, is all true, but not the flying, we can jump higher and further than any human so it may appear that we can take flight, but we glide rather than fly wearing the right attire, that's why risky business is mostly done at height."

"Are we high up now? To aid your escape? Well, that explains the wailing wind."

"Are you filled with dread to use the term wailing? I would have used whistling myself, but yes, we are higher up, well slightly."

"What about garlic, or even crucifixes, can they do you harm?"

"Ha, garlic has a strong smell that I truly detest, also the allicin inside of it is a powerful antibiotic that causes me harm but wouldn't kill me, that is all myth. Crosses are mere ornaments to me. It is a fallacy that thrusting one into my face will deter me, what a joke, many poor fools have died trying that one."

"Ok, interesting, yes interesting about the garlic and crosses that is, as for the killing that's awful. What about…"

She was cut short by Giovanni entering the room at pace. He leant down towards Drago, whispered in his ear, and without revealing anything with his poker face Drago gave a single nod then waved him away.

"What…what's happened?" she asked.

"Only that I was correct. Facial recognition has shown Carlos entering the country on an assumed name. The dog has even arrived via private jet, now that's interesting and somewhat fascinating. What has that old bastard got up his sleeve," tutting while looking pensive this time, he clicked his fingers which was surprisingly loud, and beckoned Giovanni back, placed a hand on his shoulder and drew him closer. He whispered something into his ear, then Giovanni turned sharply and left the room at the same pace he had entered, "not to worry dear Lillith, sometimes you have to play dumb to catch a dumber person. The trap will be set."

"Oh, I see. Would you like me to help at all?" Lilly tried the nice card, "I could stand guard at the door if you would just release me from these restraints." she smiled and nodded encouragingly.

"Ha, this isn't dumb and dumber dear Lillith, but nice try. I'm still not sure if you're part of this charade, you might be, you might not, and I'm not willing to trust you at this point in time, if ever."

"What? Well, be like that. I'm as truthful as I have always been," they both glared at each other again, "so, as I sit here, and as you've already stated, I might be killed by you or this Carlos man. What a dilemma."

"I've already told you that you are safe…with me. With him, probably not, so yes you are rather caught between the sword and the wall."

"Well, I'll just have to wait this ride out, not that I have a choice. Will he attack soon, this Carlos person?"

"Who knows, but we remain ready and shall wait for the showdown, and when it comes dear Lillith, for it will, I fear it will be bloody and brutal…just how I like it."

"Well in that case, please continue, you know, about what you are…I mean who you are?"

"It's like this, humans can detect vibrations through sensitive skin mechanoreceptor, however, their conscious awareness of these vibrations are generally often limited, while ours are heightened to the extreme, hence our ability to sense our surroundings more clearly. That's how we detect other vampires through their unique vibration, which is more intense than humans."

"Omg, I get all of that, you're repeating yourself. I want to know about the mind reading stuff. You said you can't but how do you influence people then?" her inquisitive mind demanded.

"Ah that, yes, I hum a hypnotic theme which is akin to a truth serum, and they mostly tell me whatever I whisper in their ear, that's how I supposedly read minds. Yet, vampiress' use a completely different tone, they use entrancing melodies that enter their victims' minds, almost similar to Celtic new age singing, and I must say it is very beautiful. It's hypnosis via singing or speaking to them telepathically, but mind reading is another thing altogether. Telepathically whispering to humans may seem like a voice in their heads, or is it me trying to compel them, to manipulate them? Some can be so easily directed to do things, and there have been stories through history of people hearing voices in their heads, well mostly they are schizophrenic, but on the few occasions they are being exploited by a vampire. You can mostly say they have gone bat shit crazy, pardon the pun."

"You seem to like your puns don't you."

"Ha, yes it seems. Yet, little do humans know that sudden touch of displaced air, or a dismissed movement witnessed on their peripheral vision, the corner of your eye as such, yes, that might be me, stalking the streets of Naples. I had a priest vampire hunter come after me two centuries past, spurting nonsense that we all go through purgatory before heaven, and if the sin is not too abhorrent, as we all have sinned, then on entering paradise we will all carry the scares of fire. But for some there will never be any redemption, the fool said it wasn't for the likes of me and that I will burn in hell forever and ever. He waved a crucifix at me, splashed holy water, leaving me no choice but to grab him by the neck, tell him that he was being absurd, then I drained him to death as he was becoming bothersome. Yes, I sometimes kill for survival, whereas humans do it for their own perverse pleasure and justify that need under the umbrella of religion but killing is what I do…when I must."

"That's just awful, you murdering him. Why kill him? He was just a fool. Are you some kind of Devil?"

"Ha, as the Devil is misunderstood, so are we. For he, Beelzebub, don't you just love that name, dared mention God may have got it wrong with you warlike violent humans, and we for hunting the rotten within your species. We ALL live in a world where one hunts the other, it's just a fact of nature and if you want to believe in a higher power, the super entity that you attach the word God to, then understand that if it lives it will be cultivated or hunted for consumption è così che è. We are not 'evil' for is the Lion evil? The Bear or the Leopard? No, it is about survival." they stared intensely at one another.

***

The muggy night continued, with what seemed an almost airless room determined to half suffocate those within. It was totally unnecessary to contain the growing rank smell of decay and fetid body sweat leading Lilly to think, *'Why doesn't someone just open a bloody window,'* but that would involve forcefully removing the nailed slats that barricaded them inside from the night outside. But, before she could put in a letter of complaint, Brody began to stir, leaving those in the room to somewhat groan at the thought of him moaning about his pain; sure enough, he started.

"Oh no, this isn't a nightmare, holy fuck it's real, the pain aargh the pain. You, get me some pain killers…" he snapped in a demanding tone at Giovanni, then on noticing Drago eyeballing him with what seemed a menacing stare he changed his tone, "errr…aargh…the pain, can you please get me something to stop the pain…please."

"Bare me the theatrics," hissed Drago, nodding at Giovanni which was an order for him to gag Brody, "I've witnessed men carry their own severed arm, even replace a mangled helmet back on their head, but on reflection he probably didn't realise part of his skull was missing. Once upon a time I became extremely skilled at impalement; would you like to experience that kind of excruciating pain?" Brody just closed his eyes and said nothing while he was harshly gagged, "no, I thought not, so stop with your bleating for what you have suffered is negligible. Now if you don't mind, please excuse me as I must attend to my waiting guests, I may appear a monster to you, but I have strong sexual needs that must be met, and they will be becoming impatient for me to join them. I will leave you here to think about what I have so far told you dear Lillith, as I am aware it is a lot for you to digest. But what I have told you is the complete truth for I have no need to lie. You could accompany me if you would like to, or perhaps you would prefer to just watch Brody in his continual suffering. I could show you some of the arts of seduction that you young Americans so lack, but that just sounds all wrong as you are my daughter."

"Derr, no thanks," replied Lilly, "who are these so called 'guests' that you spoke about?"

"Ah yes, they are what are called tobusexuals, humans that are attracted to vampires. Oh, and before you ask, I prefer any gender."

"I wasn't going to." she softly snorted in answer.

"Sometimes, I wished I were a mere mosquito that would float in and suck blood. But believe it or not, there are extremely skilled vampire hunters which are very good, hence why I can't be like the mosquito, I must be so very careful. My security is a matter of priority, for to hunt the hunter who is already hunting is extremely dangerous, and I will need all of my strength, after my needs are first met, for Carlos will be here soon, that you can be sure of." Drago turned, gave a nod to Giovanni, then left in a blink of the eye.

"So, backstabber it's just us then aye? Can I have some water please, backstabber."

"I'mah not'ah backahstabberah," Giovanni spoke with a heavy Italian accent but for our sakes it will be written in plain English, "I serve my master Drago, so therefore it is you that is the fool to have entrusted in some random stranger so quickly. If you continue in attempting to insult me, I shall gag you like him and just concentrate on the camera monitors instead, the choice is yours."

"Hmmm, ok, you just had me really convinced, a bit like that programme 'The Traitors' on TV."

"I'm not aware of that programme, but convincing is what I do, now do you want water or not?"

"Yes, but can you please just undo my restraints so I can go to the bathroom."

"The bathroom you say, you're sitting on it."

"Sorry, what are you on about? Sitting on it? What the hell are you talking about?"

"Signorina Lillith, do you honestly think Drago or I, are that stupid. Have you not noticed you and that fool are both wearing gowns? It's not for fashion, it's to cover your modesties while you urinate or worse. You are both sat on a commode, and quite why ransom films you often see don't use this tactic I shall never know. Can I use the toilet some say, they are released, there is an altercation, then the hostage escapes. A very unprofessional thing to do, no."

"You...you just want me to piss myself?"

"No young lady, just urinate and it will collect in the chamber pot, then I will empty it. It is that simple. As for the water, we will carry on as usual, I pour, you drink."

"You bunch of snakes, an answer for everything."

"No, just us being cautious is all. Now, do you want that water?"

"Yes...please," she drank, he gently dabbed her mouth with a clean cloth, then she continued, "how did you first meet him, I mean, what's the story with you and him?"

"That is between he and I, none of your business."

"Oooh, sensitive, ok, tell me more about him, I mean how does he live, how does he survive? Is he a good 'master' to you?"

"I have already mentioned, regarding he and I, it is none of your business. All I shall say is that I'm his familiar, what vampires call their closest, and he is good to me. Then there are his underlings which are many, that answer to me."

"Favouritism aye, get you. Are you lovers?" she asked curiously.

"That is between he and I."

She was about to tease him, but changed her mind mid-thought, *'Oh, yeah let me practice my mind talking,'* she considered, *'it's way too difficult when the 'master' is present.'*

[Can you hear me backstabber] there was no reaction from Giovanni, he just continued to do whatever he was doing [can you not hear me, think me, whatever this thing is I'm attempting to do. The buzzing is low level so you must surely feel something] she propelled into his head. Then to her utter surprise Giovanni answered vocally.

"Yes, I heard you in my mind."

"Why didn't you answer the first time, did I do it wrong?"

"No, you did it right, but I've already told you not to call me a backstabber."

[How sensitive you are Giovanni, then I will woo you with some…what did he say about vampiress' Enya singing lalalaaalalalaaa…]

"Nice try Lillith, but I'm used to mind talk. It's the inexperienced that are seduced and overcome with it."

"Damn," she complained, "ok, tell me about you?"

"No, I am none of your business."

"Ok, ok, take a chill pill, well…if not, tell me more about Drago, I'm curious."

"What do you mean by curious?"

"I mean, how can he literally live here right under the Neapolitans noses for all these years, no centuries? Damn he's been hiding in plain sight for so long."

"No, never hiding, he's just very smart. You see your father, I mean Drago, was called Dracula for many centuries, and realised that he needed to find a way and means to maintain a constant supply of blood as he needs to feed on a regular basis, similar to you needing to eat food. So, to not only avoid that vengeful mob carrying pitchforks and torches ablaze, he had to also avoid vampire hunters, they really do exist. Because collectively, likeminded humans are quite good at killing vampires. All this had to be done without killing or changing his targets, and definitely without raising suspicion."

"Alright, but tell me, has he ever been discovered? You know, has anyone tried to oust him as such?"

"He mentioned that in his early days, more like centuries, things were quite complex and confusing. Yet, when he finally got to grips with it, all was ok, and then a great thing happened, blood banks appeared. Through his contacts within a company that ran blood donations, he began paying a very high price for supplies of blood over many years. However, this was proving a risky business due to bureaucratic law changes, so with that in mind Drago came up with an ingenious idea of opening a tattoo studio. He designed a specific tattoo that hid the bite marks and could be placed on any part of the body, so not typically placed on the neck, although a few have had it very low on the jugular vein."

"Wow but how would a tattoo studio help him? I mean…just…can you describe the tattoo."

"Amongst his underlings it wasn't just a fashionable symbol, it became a statement to them in Naples and the south of Italy, to hide the bite. Do you remember when I mentioned to you and him," he nodded at Brody, "to go and see the tattoo shop, but he was extremely hesitant and suspicious."

"Why yes, I remember, he was so resistant to go, and dismissive to the idea."

"Well, it would have been easier for you if you did, Drago might have been able to work you out without all of this taking place, you know, the kidnapping, no abduction side of things but here we are."

[Yes, I was excited to see the studio, and possibly to have one done. Brody played me like a fiddle damn him, like you said, 'but here we are'] "Sorry, did you receive that?" asked Lilly, Giovanni nodded, "I had to try it again. It's truly weird, but I'm sure I'll get the hang of it sooner rather than later."

"Yes indeed. Do you still want to know more about Drago?" she nodded so he continued, "the tattoo parlour worked well with just enough to feed off, to satisfy his needs, yet not enough to kill. Don't forget the sheer delight and alure of the bite itself which injects a form of venom, leaving a claiming scent and taste for other vampires to avoid, he did mention they are extremely territorial. This fluid also calms the pain of the bite with an incredible euphoria, it's just amazing. You know, it actually speeds up natural revitalisation which helps with all kinds of things."

"Could you describe the sensation to me," she saw the strained look on Giovanni's face, like he couldn't be bothered, "look, if he is who he says he is I'd just like to know more about him, as much as I can. I mean what else have I to do but wait for the so-called fireworks to start aye."

Giovanni paused, his head ever so slightly dropped as if in deep thought, then he continued.

"Not that I know myself, but other underlings that take drugs have likened it to the first sensation of crack cocaine. That is all I know and the only thing for you to understand."

"Ok, ok, what about the studio is it far?"

"Well, it's not around the corner from here, more in the old town off the Via Duomo. The tattoo studio is in a dark poorly lit building tucked away from the usual tourist spots. It's above another studio, and on the second floor beside the twisting narrow streets, a perfect site for his business. The grubby, pocked marked walls, coated with graffiti serve as cover for his real intentions, alongside the tattooing that he has mastered over the years. The only downside, while he works on the tattoos, is that when he smells their blood it obviously heightens his senses and takes great effort for him to self-control his needs. When he works there, obviously at night, he has me as company."

Lilly looked at him, uncomfortably interested in what he was telling her, but at the end of the day he was still serving a monster. Still wildly disorientated with the whole situation, the surrealness of it all seemed to make her mind float within itself as she focussed her waning eyes on Giovanni again, he continued.

"The tattoo studio sometimes attracts the interest of the many tourists that visit Naples, and it has become beneficial to Drago, as a change in flavour can be exiting. And as the tattoo is designed to hide the bite mark it's a dream come true, a somewhat gift, as hundreds of people worldwide now have one, and becoming quite fashionable amongst us."

"But surely that couldn't raise enough revenue, I mean…surely not."

"No, true enough, real estate, investments, Drago also supplies drugs to the customers that come through his door. These drugs he supplies are used to hook in some of his victims, one to keep them compliant while feeding off them and two to maintain their addiction so they keep returning to him for their next much needed fix, plus the venom. Drago has contact with a main drug dealer here in Naples, and through his many deals he has managed to procure and maintain a constant supply. He offers protection for the head dealer who pays a huge amount for that said protection and to ward off any other gangs that attempt to takeover. The majority of Drago's customers are young men and women who are not the most perfect people of society, being unemployed, living off state handouts, and needing a next fix. This works for Drago as this means he can get regularly fed with their blood and ensure their return for the drugs he supplies. He preys on their vulnerability, knowing they are desperate, and has mastered doctoring the strength and potency of the drug when he wants to feed. You see, he likes to get high now and again on the blood of drug addicts, but now I must leave you, Drago will be back at night fall."

"What are you going to leave us here all day?"

"Yes, until sunset. Drago has gone to eventually rest and will be back later. You will have adequate water to keep you both hydrated, just suck on that tube," he pointed at tubes beside their heads, "when he gets back there will be more to discuss and plan for the arrival of Carlos."

The arrival of Carlos
Chapter 7

six months earlier

THE ONLY SOUND to be heard came from the tap of an immaculate cane, that was used by the apparently sophisticated man. It was only on closer inspection you might notice the fraying edge of his shirt collar, accompanied with faint stains dotted along his sleeve and a faded salt residue circle on the back of his scruffy suit, all topped off with a Panama hat which had slight grease stains around the rim. He was of an average height with dark curly hair which had smatterings of grey flecks running through it and worn long around the ears; to hide the fact he is missing the top part of the left one due to it being ripped off in a violent ambush many years ago. The stern-faced man sported a moustache that he oiled daily, with curls at the ends of it as he thinks it makes him look distinguished; a bit like the fictional famous Belgian detective Hercule Poirot. If you passed him in the street one would assume he was a middle-aged tired looking businessman who had seen better days, carrying a rotund barrel shaped torso and a beer belly paunch from eating too many rich meals. Regardless of his appearance he was a powerful man that walked with a pronounced limp, a leg which was damaged from being bitten during the same altercation with what ripped off part of his ear. Now having to use a cane to walk, it gave him the excuse to hide a blade that was kept honed to perfection and made of solid silver. If it were unsheathed, it would be smooth and deadly especially to the things he hunted, and a perfect slash could potentially remove a head in one strike. He had spent many years perfecting this technique, training with swordsmen from around the world with many other unscrupulous people, not unlike himself.

He was a rather unpleasant man, sneaky and unpredictable, having no family, never wanting to marry or have children, and preferred to be alone; it was better that way for him, and his way of life. If he felt himself needing the company of a woman, he had plenty of contacts to choose from, but he had a weird sexual fetish which he went to great measures in making sure his desperate 'guests' kept confidential, making them give their word on disclosing anything, to ensure his privacy. But as we all know, verbal agreements aren't worth the paper they're not printed on, as the poor unfortunate women made him pay handsomely for the pain inflicted upon them, and for not blackmailing him in not going to the police.

This man is known as Carlos.

***

Carlos entered the bar he liked to frequent during evenings in Buenos Aires, Argentina. It was small, discreet, and thankfully an airconditioned place which served his favourite meal of Asado and red wine. On finishing his meal, and on the start of a second bottle of a rather fine Malbec, he was approached by a man who he had noticed was looking at him. Carlos griped his ever-present cane, ready to decapitate or kill if necessary.

"Buenas noches, pueda acompanarte?" (Good evening, may I join you?) the man asked.

"Si, puedes, como puedo ayudarte?" (Yes, you may, how can I help you?) Carlos replied displaying a calm persona but was on high alert.

"I'm sorry, but do you speak any English, as my Spanish is a little rusty?"

"Si, yes of course Senor, join me, take a seat, I haven't seen you around before, are you here on vacation?" Carlos quizzed offering the man the seat next to him with an opened palm gesture, while man introduced himself as…

"I am Mr Venator."

"And I am Carlos," he gave the man an extremely hard handshake, one to assert his dominance and the second to hold his attention by keeping the hand clasped while he asked, "Venator, si, isn't that Latin for hunter?"

"Why yes, you surprise me for being so well read. Yes, I am a hunter by name, and a hunter by nature. It's something I have done for most of my life having grown up in the country of the sadly forgotten era of apartheid, South Africa."

Carlos' interest was now piqued by Mr Venator, over the 'hunter' statement, and as the evening went on, they both moved from wine to tequila and continued to drink while they discussed many topics.

After dancing around the main subject which Mr Venator really wanted to discuss and never offered a first name which Carlos found slightly strange, he mentioned being a procurer and revealed that he was also a trophy hunter. His passion was collecting the heads of wild animals and curiosities from all around the world and then moved closer to Carlos as if he were to divulge a secret.

"You see Carlos, the piece de resistance for my collection would be the glory of having the head of a vampire mounted on my wall. It's an ambition, no, a lifelong aim, to add this extraordinarily rare piece to my collection."

This totally surprised the unsuspecting Carlos who was unaware that the man he shared a bottle of tequila with already knew of him, for why make that statement.

"What makes you think they are real? Let alone exist?"

Mr Venator told him of his thorough, long extensive research, then went onto say that he had discovered who Carlos was, and that he was indeed a vampire hunter. Perhaps it was the alcohol that made Carlos begin to talk, or the huge ego he carried around on his shoulders, but he found himself divulging much to Mr Venator who sat closely beside him, declaring that he was in fact a world-renowned vampire hunter, well…in an extremely limited circle, and that he had made it his life's mission to eradicate the world of these evil monstrous beings. Through the smoky haze of the cigars they had lit, Carlos began to explain that vampires are supremely elusive and almost impossible to find, as they have spent centuries attempting to stay hidden, out of view, but lived in plain sight within their own territories, using their various networks of either paid or unpaid underlings to do their bidding.

"You see Mr Venator, it was just by chance, or twisted fate, that I discovered all of this. Innocent, oblivious humans were ignorantly living amongst vampires. There was one right here, that I had discovered, who had left the old world and headed for South America, mainly Argentina, a bit like the Nazis after the war. How many moved here nobody knows, they prefer it as the Southern Hemisphere normally has slightly less daylight than the Northern side," Carlos stared at Mr Venator, unsure if he should reveal what happened, then couldn't help himself, "it was a fresh vampire, less than a hundred years old, so was still ignorant to how conniving some of us humans can be, mainly myself, and that was the first I discovered, and the first I dispatched."

This revelation upped the tempo as Mr Venator wasn't sure if Carlos was drunk bullshitting, but he was running out of time and had nothing to lose, so reached down and lifted a crusty old brown leather bag which Carlos presumed carried clothing and dirty underwear, then placed it on the table in front of them both. Carlos looked at the bag, then back at Mr Venator who nodded at it.

"That is for you."

On inspecting the contents, after clumsily sliding the zip across which got stuck but with a sharp tug got going again, Carlos showed great control by not letting his mouth drop while Mr Venator continued.

"Fifty thousand dollars for our conversation tonight, and if you help me with my quest, you will receive ten million dollars when the job is done and an expense account you could only dream of having. You will be allowed to run it into the millions. But and I must stress this emphatically, I must have the vampire alive, for I, and only I must take the vampire's head."

Now, Carlos wasn't a stupid man, but he was greedy, and the money offered was mind blowing, so he sat quietly and just stared at Mr Venator who stared back.

"Once you start this ball rolling there is no going back," Carlos said while griping Mr Venator's arm rather aggressively, "my line of work is not only dangerous to the extreme but can cost many lives. Do you understand."

"Yes, I understand," he replied, then tugged at and lifted Carlos' strong grip from his arm, "I want this to be done as quickly as possible, I must have the vampire alive as soon as possible."

"Quickly you say. It is my job to draw them out from wherever they are hidden, yes, but as a matter of fact, I do have intel on a particular vampire in Naples. One that you will proudly adorn your walls with its head. But one that is extremely dangerous and may cost the lives of much manpower."

"Why Naples? Why not one closer?"

"Who is the vampire hunter, me or you," Carlos said aggressively, "you haven't even asked the name of that one!"

"And the name of that one is…" Mr Venator asked not being concerned or bothered, he just wanted a vampire but was stunned to the core when Carlos said...

"That one is the one and only…Dracula."

Both men stared at each other intensely, the excitement rose within them, almost chocking them for they couldn't believe their luck. Mr Venator for possibly getting a not so mythical vampire, just the most famous of them all, and Carlos for manoeuvring it to the one he wanted, desperately craving revenge after all these years.

"If what you are saying is true my friend, I think we could be of great use to each other, but I need actual proof of what you are telling me. You do understand, don't you?"

"Of course, if you want, I can show you, I live not far from here. Come if you like and you can see my evidence." Carlos offered.

Mr Venator had one more question for Carlos, a very important one that everything depended on.

"Tell me Carlos, just humour me before we go, but is it just a childish story of horror tales, or can the blood from a vampire truly give immortality to whoever drinks it?"

"What?" Carlos snapped, bemused at the question, "are you mad? The price for immortality is eternal damnation, to become the undead is pure sacrilege don't you see. But yes, there are myths and stories that the blood of a true vampire might give immortality to whomever is foolish enough to drink it, but it is not a risk I would be willing or prepared to take. The effects I'm told are horrendous pain before death, as only a handful from thousands can be converted. But I suppose there are some mad delusional fools out there who would be willing to try. I don't think you quite understand, they are evil to the core, nothing about them is good. This is not the movies Mr Venator." Carlos sneered.

***

They walked the short distance to Carlos's apartment in silence, both deep in thought. When they arrived, Mr Venator had to hide his mixture of utter amazement and bemusement at the condition of the place. The walls were covered from floor to ceiling with graphs and charts, it was almost a shrine to the obsessiveness of Carlos's quest to find the vampires he was seeking to destroy.

"It was rumoured that a vampire had travelled with the conquistadores in the 16th century being part of the expedition," Carlos began his boastful story, "he was associated with Pedro de Mendoza, who founded the city of Buenos Airies in 1536, it was then known as Tucuman. Together the troops had explored, fought and conquered parts of the Americas. Now that particular vampire had fed on many humans, and even with all the hundreds of thousands that he killed only a few were changed successfully. You see, they become bored over time, then begin to enjoy the thrill of being chased. Maybe immortality becomes a heavy cross of suffering on their shoulders, an immense burden to carry. When you've done everything, seen everything, experienced virtually everything possible, what do you do then, how do you enjoy the excitement again? It became a deadly game of cat and mouse as he hid, then I found him again, he was enjoying the 'chase me if you can' game that had begun between us. You see, mostly all vampires are self-centred and think we humans are as dumb as a cow, and on discovering that weakness of theirs I used it to my advantage. Eventually he slipped up out of conceitedness and contempt, then I found and killed him fast, the second to my tally. You must be very fast and not lose the element of surprise to kill them, it's the only way. It's surprising on death how their bodies decompose into a mush, then dry into dust, a true sight to witness I must say. But if you were to behead one, a strong formaldehyde solution should do the trick in preserving it."

"You've actually killed one?"

"Two."

"I mean I thought you were bullshitting earlier…what I mean is…you've actually fucking done it?"

"Do not play with me Mr Venator, you know I'm deadly serious," Carlos drew his sword, and with intense light shining off its extremely sharp point, swished it nipping Mr Venator's neck, "this is not a game, I have actually fucking done it, yes."

They glared intensely at each other, with neither wanting to blink first. Carlos had made the earlier conscious decision not to inform him of his previous encounter with Dracula, for fear of not being hired, but now he began to panic, thinking he had pushed it too far with the slight neck in his neck. He was now desperate on getting the job, becoming fearful in losing it, so he blinked first and leaned closer to Mr Venator and quietly said.

"I apologise, please forgive me, I am just so very passionate about my job."

"I understand, just don't do that again." Mr Venator said through gritted teeth as the sound of crunching metallic clicks from behind his jacket demonstrated the uncocking of a gun.

They continued with a slight air of contention, that violent men do when they need the help from someone they don't trust, looking at information and historical facts all about Naples and where the vampire they sought may possibly be hiding. There were images of the tomb of Vlad the Impaler, inside the cloister of Santa Maria la Nova, a 13th century church, where it is now claimed the Dracula was entombed. Mr Venator thought that Carlos was a complete lunatic with an unhealthy obsession and needed to get out more, but he proved to be a genius regarding vampires and just the man he needed for this dangerous mission. He guessed that only time would tell, but if he obtained what he was after he would be immensely satisfied.

"I can see you have been extremely thorough in your research; how long have you been working on this?" he questioned Carlos.

"As I said before, for many years, and I feel now that I have some concrete evidence of a living child of a vampire, would you like to see for yourself, the results of the DNA test I procured?"

A section of one of the walls was covered with notes, charts and various photographs of Lillith from her High School photos to her Graduation Ceremony, her driving license and passport details. To where she worked and socialised, it was a timeline of her life, and in the centre was pinned the DNA results which in Carlos' mind was the proof that there was a strong link to the vampire that he wanted to kill so badly.

"Who is that? Is she a vampire?"

"No, the potential daughter of one, possibly, and before you ask that pathetic question again, no, her blood is diluted and cannot give extended life. One of my past accomplices tried and nothing happened, which was good for him as I would have killed him if he converted, the fool just felt sick for a month after losing the lining of his stomach. No, it must be pure vampire blood, but like I've already mentioned, you would have to be a complete and utter fool to try."

"So, it can't work with half breed blood, it has to be true vampire blood?"

"Stop asking that stupid question, are you deaf, why do you persist? I have already told you that half breed blood is worthless to humans but supposedly dangerous to vampires. Now listen, I also have some information you might find interesting, through extensive research I have discovered that this Dracula could be connected to this girl in New York, possibly his daughter, so you can either have the head of a half breed or the real thing, but I'll need the half breed alive to lure out the real deal. Just think, the most famous trophy could be hanging on your wall."

Mr Venator feigned interest in what Carlos was telling him, he just wanted a vampire, any vampire and didn't careless about a daughter, but the lure thing sounded good so encouraged Carlos to continue.

"Please continue, I need to know more, this is truly unbelievable. I have been seeking someone as yourself for a while now; to finally have the ultimate prize within my grasp is something I thought I would never be able to achieve. But prey tell me, how did you first find out where Dracula was? How is that even possible?"

Carlos's ego was becoming rather inflated and with the added lubricant of alcohol, he began to naively confide in him.

"My research led me down many various and treacherous paths, and I used my many contacts from all around the world to aid me in my quest," after taking a good gulp of his drink Carlos continued, "you see, I started by checking the records of all the women who had died in childbirth, mostly between 21 and 23 years ago and went back 9 months to find out where they were when they fell pregnant. I successfully managed to narrow it down to a woman called Adele who had visited Naples and had died giving birth to a daughter named Lillith, the dates all matched up."

"What has that got to do with Dracula?"

"A lure is all we can do to draw him out, so I needed bait, do you get it now, it's something he might want. It's all about research, research, research. I then instructed some of my more salubrious Dark Web internet hackers to source any information on this girl, you know, where she lives and who with, her educational history and her medical records and so forth, all this accumulated information led me to believe that this girl maybe a dhampir, which to you may seem nothing but in layman's terms she is a child of a vampire. Now, that would make her a rarity, an almost once in a lifetime event. So, to confirm my suspicions, I orchestrated a fake blood and DNA test to be emailed to her, it offered an 80% discount, a too tempting offer for her to refuse, and she took the dangling carrot, ha. When the results came back, voila, all the pieces of the jigsaw had come together."

Mr Venator nodded enthusiastically, turned to look at Carlos, and with a wolfish grin said.

"I think I have found my true vampire hunter, I can tell this is your life's work, and to finally be within the grasp of having the monsters head for my collection is a dream come true. You are most definitely the man for the job. We will obviously need to have several more meetings to confirm and fine tune the details, but if you are satisfied with my very generous offer, that I have proposed to you earlier, I would be delighted if you would work for me in fulfilling my quest."

Carlos turned back to look at the wall of charts in front of him.

"This won't be an easy task you know as they are extremely skilled at concealment, are you sure you are ready for this? For on embarking with this hunt? Please understand that it will have to be done exactly as I say," Carlos paused, "you know there is a tale that Vlad who became Dracula once declared to the Sultan Mehmed the second that 'All bridges between us are broken, and I am waiting for you on my ground'. So, we will be on his ground so it MUST be done my way right, do you understand." Carlos forcefully stamped his terms.

"I understand." Mr Venator zealously replied.

"They are extremely difficult to shoot as their hearing and senses are amazingly astute. We will have to develop a dart to carry silver dust, it must be virtually noiseless, like the wings of an owl compared to other birds. Vampires are extremely sensitive in high levels of silver which causes them breathing problems, it incapacitates them quickly. We must prepare; we must get ready for the hunt."

***

Over the coming months Carlos had several meetings with Mr Venator, either through video calls or face to face meetings to fine tune all the plans in trapping and behead Dracula. There would be no stone left unturned, this mission had to be perfect and foolproof down to the last tiniest detail.

Although Carlos was based in Argentina, he also has a cheap rundown apartment in New York which he uses for his various 'business meetings', and this is where he held most of his meetings with Mr Venator, or through zoom if he wasn't available. He had been given Carte Blanche to fund and recruit his team to seek out the vampire and enlisted a crew of ruthless mercenaries that was suggested to him by his new employer. A team of ex Black Operatives, that Mr Venator had worked with in the past on other missions, were to accompany him to Naples. Carlos also rehired the adonis Brody to befriend Lillith to be used as bait.

It was a few weeks before the planned rendezvous in Naples. Carlos was in his office with Brody explaining and going over the details yet again as he was questioning Carlos' authority.

"Brody, just do the job I am paying you to do. Your objective is Lillith and getting her to Naples. I'll leave the finer details on how you achieve this in your more than capable hands, just do not seduce her. Look at her photo, it's hard to believe she is a...she is stunning is she not," Carlos smirked at Brody, knowing him too well, "your 'placement' at the museum starts on Monday, she takes her lunch there most days at 1pm, so be there ready to do your stuff."

Carlos slid a folder over the desk which held the relevant details about Lillith, it contained her school and college information, where she lived, liked to eat and shop, dating, but not her family history.

"What is so important about this Lillith? Who is she anyway?" Brody quizzed.

"All you need to know is that she is vital to this assignment, just get her there and keep her safe, got it?"

"You really need to get a life Carlos; all this is getting out of control man."

Carlos was rapidly losing patience with Brody, he had a long and tiresome video call with Mr Venator to fine tune and double check all the details, going over and over them until they both knew and understood what was required of them all.

"Just do the job I am paying you very handsomely for, and stop whining and worrying, it's a straightforward assignment, just get her to Naples, and leave the rest to me."

He explained yet again to Brody of what his role in all of this, and to ensure she was to be kept completely unaware of anything until the mission was complete. Brody was also kept in the dark and unaware, that a particular vampire was to be presented to Mr Venator. If Lillith was to sadly die during the hunt, then so be it, for the main objective was to kill the Vampire, then Brody could skulk back to New York, or wherever, and receive his blood money; then wait for his next assignment. Carlos shuffled the papers in front of him, looked up at Brody and with a dismissive wave snapped.

"Our meeting here is finished, so leave," Carlos continued in his belligerent, assertive attitude towards Brody, "I have a few loose ends to tie up before we meet in Naples, and do not forget I will keep in contact with you regularly. Your burner phones will be delivered to you later tonight, and I don't have to remind you to keep them fully charged and on you at all times, do I, no, and don't forget what I told you about the trackers, it is vitally important. Do not fuck this up do you hear."

Carlos had instructed Brody to always carry several tracker devices on him, and to plant them on anyone who approached or made conversation with them at any time, and he is to trust no one. Brody raised his hands and eyebrows at Carlos.

"Ok, ok I know, I'm not an idiot."

"Well, that has yet to be proven doesn't it Brody, remember Colorado? The next time I see you we will be in Naples, enjoy your time getting acquainted with the delicious Lillith, and remember our time plan is two weeks, so get schmoozing with her but no sex. You tend to have your way then leave, so no sex and I mean that, this has to go to plan understand. I'm sure that won't be too much of a task for your simple brain to comprehend. So, as they say in Naples, Ciao."

***

Brody left Carlos's office, mulling over what he had been told and how it was to be done.

"Man-oh-man." He muttered under his breath.

This was going to be a tough job, and he was kind of sure he could pull it off. The problem was that Lillith was a looker, and he had already been warned by Carlos not to bed her. Still, when the sting was over, he'd definitely give it a go. He trotted down the plain dimly lit stairs as his stomach rumbled with hunger, with the thought of all the delicious pizzas and pastries he could sample in Naples.

On hearing Brody tap-dance down the stairs Carlos sat back in his grubby soft blood red leather chair and took a deep breath while massaging his temples. That would be their last face to face meeting until they rendezvoused in Naples, for the final part of the assignment. He felt confident he had wisely chosen Brody for this job, his handsome looks and abilities in charming women, even men, would be perfect. His only concern was that Brody might get side tracked, he sometimes had the attention span of a gnat when it came to important details, yet with all the will in the world, he was sure he had drummed the importance of this assignment into him enough times. He was fully aware that Brody would just be collateral damage if it went wrong; he is what is known as the lights are on but nobody's home type of man. And of Lillith, well she is just a half-blood and not a pure blood, so if she were to die during the operation, then so be it. In his mind it would still be erasing one more monster from the world, even if it was a half-blood vampire.

Carlos had studied past details on where Drago could possibly have been, places he might have frequented and attempted a process of elimination on his every move. He had past extensive evidence of where he stalked, and like his apartment in Argentina, Carlos' office wall was full of facts and information that must have had some rhyme or reasoning to them, but not to anyone else. With this he triangulated where he wanted Brody to steer Lillith, so there was a 'chance' meeting. Brody was instructed to take Lilly out in the evenings and guide her directly towards the Spanish quarter as he knew that was where Drago often went at night, the old town would be the second choice.

***

After Carlos killed his first vampire, he extensively travelled the world, diligently researching historical places and sourcing information from various books. He listened to the tales that some told and gathered details from so-called eyewitnesses who swore they had experienced a vampire. Most leads hit a dead-end, crashing into the wall of fantasy, but on the very rare occasion he struck gold. Carlos was a brutal man when he got going, a hard man, who let nothing stop him achieving his goals. Even if that meant the killing of innocent people caught in the crossfire of deceit and were unintentionally or intentionally mistaken through gossip and lies of being a vampire.

He had briefly considered, for this assignment, in contacting a fellow vampire hunter who was based there in New York to assist with this hunt. They had worked together many years ago in Louisiana on a hunt for a particularly vicious female vampire, a Soucouyant in Caribbean folklore, that had arrived from Trinidad. But that conniving vampire hunter took all the glory by taking the teeth of said vampire as a trophy which infuriated Carlos, for amongst the exceptionally small circle of hunters, that two-faced New Yorker took all the credit. Now however, Carlos's inflated ego dissuaded him from making contact, even though that hunter supposedly had eight kills to his name and was extremely experienced. For Carlos' vanity and ego would take the full glory of ridding the earth finally of Dracula. So, on considering that memory, it only reminded him to do otherwise, for the kudos of such a great catch shall be his, and his alone. Because, on hearing the news of Dracula's death through their grape vine of damnation, the other vampires will go to ground and suck on vermin like the sewer rats they are. But, the memory of his first encounter with Dracula had caused a post-traumatic stress disorder to rise within him, for during that encounter many years ago he barely escaped with his life. He was close to being killed by that monster, losing the top part of his ear which he covers with hair and also received a bite that ripped into a nerve causing him to forever limp in pain. He lost three men in that attempt at killing Dracula, tough men, good men. So, Carlos had to put his arrogance and rudeness aside, concentrating more on his sneaky conniving traits, a bit like a well-known American Politian. This time he was not only going to capture him, but he was also going to witness it's killing through beheading.

***

The flight arrived in Naples during the day, where Carlos travelled under an assumed identity by using a false passport knowing how far and wide Dracula's network stretched. He tried his damnedest to make it as difficult as possible in being detected so he had flown in on a private plane, that had been organised by Mr Venator, to bypass any unwanted attention from airport staff. So, to say he was paranoid of the slightest thing going wrong was an understatement. He stepped outside the plane and was assailed by the heat, sounds and smells and could not wait getting to his hotel, unpack, and get started with the mission. The five mercenaries he had travelled with were to stay in a separate location, so as not to raise any unnecessary suspicion, and loaded their luggage into a blacked-out minibus that was waiting for them on the tarmac; the other mercenaries will join them later when they arrive on Mr Venator's flight. Carlos was becoming slightly concerned as Brody hadn't answered the burner phone, but the location tracker he sneaked into his passport placed Brody at the hotel, so he sent one of the mercenaries to check.

Meanwhile, all the other location trackers which were craftily placed by Brody, responded clearly so Carlos presumed he had done his job correctly. The signals allowed for coordinates to be cross-checked and triangulated, Carlos was quite analytical, while the other mercenaries tailed the unsuspecting targets to eliminate them from the list of suspects. Most of the emphasis was placed in finding Giovanni, for his location tracker would no doubt lead him to the deadliest catch.

***

Shortly after Mr Venator had arrived, with his band of sadistic mercenaries come bodyguards, that were built like brick out houses. On arriving at the hotel he began displaying an incredible level of arrogance by showing a strange device to his team that wasn't previously agreed upon.

"What is that?" asked Carlos.

"Don't worry yourself, it's just a weapon I've had engineered to be used by one of the snipers."

"Well, that is evident, it doesn't look like a weaponised form of water pistol, full of crushed and diluted antibiotics that helps wreak havoc which I advised you on getting. Silver dust in liquid form will incapacitate him yes, but he not only needs to be incapacitated as quickly as possible but must remain that way."

"I thought I'd down one bird with two stones as such, silver dust…and this."

"But what is that? I have told you that everything must go as I have planned. There must be no deviation from what was agreed, do you not understand."

Mr Venator handed the strange looking weapon over to a mercenary, nodded at him and watched him leave the room.

"Look, I understand your demands Carlos, but sometimes situations must. I have to be sure in what you have claimed regarding its existence, with the blood being tested."

"This is not just a wild off the wall claim my friend, they do exist you fool."

"Give us the room," Mr Venator said to his men as he watched them leave, "listen hear Carlos, it is my money that is funding this hunt and don't you forget it," they both glared at each other, with the sound of Carlos grinding his teeth through rage, "look, we are both hunters and therefore passionate about what we do, so easy with the insults ok!"

You could almost feel a vein about to pop from the side of Carlos' head, his face almost bright red with anger, but he decided to calm himself as the hunt for his vampire nemesis was about to materialise.

"You have humbled me…" Carlos reeled his neck in for fear of being removed from the hunt, after all Mr Venator's men were now in charge of his equipment, "forgive me, that was wrong of me, it's just that last time I was here…"

"You don't have to explain," Mr Venator interrupted, "I already know about the encounter you had with him in the past, it was mentioned to me by another vampire hunter from New York," they continued glaring at each other, "yes, and that hunter wanted nothing to do with this hunt as he said it was far too dangerous. Oh, and it was he that put your name forward."

The intense glaring continued, and on any other day Carlos might have swished his sword from the cane and run the man in front of him through, whereas Mr Venator might have shot Carlos in the head for his insolence. But this time they needed each other, so they silently agreed to move on with the hunt as that was the most important thing at hand.

***

The team of mercenaries stealthily surrounded the perimeter where Drago might be holding Lilly and Brody, managing to snatch one of his supposed underlings hanging around in the area. They whisked him away to extract as much information as possible, almost drowning him, and then forced a bag over his head as he sat with his hands bound behind him. Carlos entered.

"Did he talk?" the two mercenaries shook their heads slowly from side to side, "we need that information, get it from him or kill I will him."

With that the bag was violently tugged from the underling's head, his face showing total fear.

"No, no more, please no more…" the underling croaked.

A hand grabbed the back of his greasy unwashed hair and forced his head into the barrel of water, that also carried the urine of the mercenaries. Moments passed as the sound of the underling's near 'death rattle' gurgled up alongside his face, then his head was forcibly jerked upwards, almost having hair pulled from the roots, with water spraying and cascading along desperately blinking eyes. The gasping underling drew in air, only to have it brutally stolen again for back into the water it went but this time it is was submerged slightly longer than the time before. An answer to a question will come or forever never leave his lips, the choice belonged to the drowning man.

With the relevant information now extracted from the underling, that had his throat slashed by Carlos even though he told them precisely what they wanted, the hunters now knew exactly how many were present and also the layout of the premises to be attacked.

"There is no room for alterations to the plan, you do understand." Carlos snapped at Mr Venator.

"Yes of course, but don't worry the plan will go ahead, the question mark is…can we catch him?"

"The answer to that I don't know any more than you, just follow the plan, that is all we can do."

Carlos just assumed he was in control of the assignment, when in fact he was being used as much as Brody was used by himself, a pawn to Mr Venator's overall plan; for he was determined to get the job done and get out of there asap.

"Let the games begin, send in the sacrificial lambs as such." Mr Venator quietly told Carlos.

The assault on Drago/Dracula
Chapter 8

THE CHAOTIC DIN of chatter resonated around the disused warehouse, intensifying around the old office area where Lilly and Brody were still being held captive. Even in her elevated state of discomfort, from not only peeing in a commode but the unbearably hot room smelling of urine and excrement from the unchanged basin, then having to sleep sitting upright leaving her with a terrible crooked neck. Lilly could clearly hear the English-speaking underlings panicking on what to do next which truly got her goat.

"Oh, for the love of…that's your only argument?" Lilly complained, "someone please pass that bucket as listening to your conversations has made me truly vomitus. That's like saying you've never had shit on the outside part of your thumb nail while wiping your ass, it happens but nobody talks about it. Defeat can happen to Drago, yet none of you morons are willing to talk about it. I don't think you're as well prepared as you might think you are. Those few were probably the cannon fodder with the worst yet to come."

Toned down hysterical cussing and arguing continued until their eyes squeezed tight from the cringe-instilling sound of nails being dragged along a steel pipe, punctured the stifling air, paralysing thoughts and crunching faces in distress, their attention had been achieved.

"What is going on?" Drago drawled with an undertone of annoyance...

Giovanni was usually measured with his comments towards Drago, but this time he had to voice his concerns sharply.

"Where have you been Drago? This is not a joke anymore, do you understand. We discovered what look like mercenaries close to the perimeter, one had even penetrated our heat sensors and reached the outer wall. When your underlings finally engaged, they were shot and some killed by sniper fire allowing for all but one of the mercenaries to escape, and that one is dead. Drago, they have not only found us but are already here and seem to be professionals."

"Don't worry yourself Giovanni, let me see the body," Drago's self-centred overconfident side shone through to Giovanni's frustration. They all simultaneously pointed at a body with its head slumped to one side after being thrown against a wall as if it were a dummy, "damn that Carlos, they must have all come straight from the airport. This one has even had trace silver injected into him, in case I bite him, look that's why he is blue greyish of skin colour. They must be being paid huge amounts of money to take this risk. Damn it, damn that Carlos, and damn you all as I needed the mercenary dog alive, how can I extract the information I need from him now?"

"While you were pleasuring yourself," Giovanni made a cutting remark, "we discovered the mercs reccying or casing the joint as such. We have been discovered Drago, but how has this happened?"

Drago looked around then stopped, it was the woman that accompanied Giovanni to coerce Lilly and Brody into joining them for dinner, allowing for the abduction.

"You come here," he commanded, "scan her Giovanni, damn that Brody must have planted a tracker on both of you, the sneaky bastard might not be as dumb as I first thought."

"Now, who's using profanities." said Lilly.

"Not now." replied Drago.

"Oh no, it is true, look," moaned a surprised Giovanni while showing the scanner bleeping, "we must move now, before it is too late, Carlos must have sent those men as a penetrating distraction, to check if you were here. We must move now!"

"Giovanni, you imbecile, you fell asleep at the wheel. I positively instructed you to check everything and everyone, you have failed me." Drago's eyes burned into Giovanni's with rage.

"But Drago…master…think about it, why did they retreat so suddenly? Did they know you weren't here? Wait, wait, did you speed yourself here…or did you walk normally?"

"I walked here normally, why wouldn't I?"

"They must have waited for your return, and now know you are here, you fool Drago, they will soon attack with force you…"

Before Giovanni could finish, he received a powerful backhanded slap from Drago, that sent him sprawling across the floor towards some of the other stunned underlings, with the gasp of a shock from Lilly coming in just as fast. Drago then looked at her with the same furious eyes and bellowed to all in the room.

"Remember who you are talking to, I have learned not to be greedy these past centuries; the days of death predation were over, with stealth becoming the word. So,

I only took what was needed without killing mostly, yet things have changed, and my thirst grows deeper, as if these self-imposed invisible chains that keep me here want to destroy my very presence through discovery. Is it the stirrings of Vesuvius that torments my blackened soul once more, as it did long ago when I went on a killing spree? Am I about to press the self-destruct button in wanting that bastard vampire hunter Carlos dead at any cost? This is his second chance gaming at cat and mouse, where I am 'supposedly' the mouse. But I am the one and only Dracula, and Carlos must die."

[That all sounds rather dramatic 'Dad'] Lilly telepathically yanked at his chain.

[I said not now Lillith] came the sharp reply.

Drago then slid a respirator over his head which he assumed would be enough against silver dust, but how wrong could he have been, for at amazingly the same time a modified tubular syringe like dart burst through a slight gap in the uneven boards that barricaded the windows, punctured his neck and filled instantly with his blood, sucking it out as if he were the victim. Then it automatically disengaged with an electronic whirling sound and headed for the floor. It was virtually a nano second after the first when another dart burst through the same gap carrying liquid silver, not dust which he had arrogantly presumed would be used. That dart Drago only just managed to hear and react to, with an attempt at swatting it away as you might the annoying buzzing sound of a mosquito, but he missed and that too punctured his neck as it partially deposited its contents. He awkwardly grabbed it, growled, and tossed it across the room, where it ricocheted off an underling and struck Brody in the head as if it were a dartboard; Brody yelped as it fully unloaded this time, his eyes wide in shock and surprise.

"AARGH," Drago yelled with a demonic sounding tone and began struggling for breath, he convulsed then crumpled to the ground.

Stunned underlings displayed signs of not knowing what to do, some reacted weirdly, with one pulling at their own hair with the onset of fear coupled with anxiety. Lilly obviously sat there, firstly looking at the collapsed thrashing Drago, and then at the dart that was sticking out of Brody's head, and before she finished saying.

"Well, this has turned into a shit show…"

All hell broke loose with an RPG being fired at the secured door, causing bits of wood and shrapnel to spray in all directions, literally like confetti thrown at a wedding. This was quickly followed by badly barricaded windows being smashed open and flash grenades tossed inside. Tear gas must have simultaneously been tossed in too, adding to the confusion of those now desperately gasping for breath.

"I knew the fool would show incredible arrogance after our last encounter," roared Carlos, "quick men, strike fast while Dracula is weak."

Carlos' hackles rose as he lifted a fist; it had all kicked off exactly to plan with a barrage of bullets taking down underlings as if a scythe were cutting down crops. Magazine clips were removed and reinserted by true professionals, fast and efficient, continuing the hail of bullets to keep the element of surprise in their favour. But, even well researched plans can go wrong, as unforeseen events can happen during bloody vicious fights as Giovanni slammed down a heavy metal pipe cracking a mercenary's skull wide open, causing blood to gush through the splintered bone showing the cerebral cortex shining through. Only a miracle could save the underlings now, but there were none to be had amongst the carnage and mayhem as Giovanni was shot in the gut. He staggered backward, collapsing onto his coccyx with a thud which joined in with the sound of continuing gunfire.

Suddenly, Drago mustered up the remnants of his strength, leaping upward and with an almighty swipe downwards, dragged his claws from top to bottom along a mercenary's face, slicing skin and bone like a hot knife through butter, removing an eye from its socket and splitting his bottom lip wide open after also splitting his nose in two. The force of the claw buried into the top of the mercenary's chest as Drago violently jerked and wrenched at his sternum, with a cracking sound finally giving way to the sight of the chest being ripped open for all to see. The brutality of that made another mercenary stop in terror, for he had witnessed and delivered much violence in his life but had never seen anything as gruesome as that. He was transfixed by what seemed red smouldering eyes, rather like the headlights of a car hurtling towards a stunned deer, and the last thing he knew was the sensation of being lifted, followed by ferocious tearing agony that escorted him into death. His body crumpled to the ground without its head, with blood gushing from the neck stump, but not before the mercenary had fired a tip exploding round that hit a bone in Drago's arm. He roared in pain as the liquid silver entered his body causing him to convulse further, to then writhe on the floor right in front of his jubilant nemesis Carlos.

All the while Lilly's reality touched on the surreal carnage before her. It seemed like a video game unfolding right there with bodies being ripped apart and falling close to her feet, with blood spraying like a shaken champagne bottle going off. Even a head bounced of her knee leaving the indent of teeth on her skin which caused a sharp sting of pain similar to a pinch, making her realise this wasn't a nightmare, this was really happening.

She watched as Carlos, stake in one hand, a pistol in the other, pounced while revelling in his excitement on wanting to kill Drago.

"Fuck them all, this kill is mine and mine alone."

Carlos couldn't be any closer to his obsession, being totally focused on the kill, so hadn't noticed Drago's accomplice Giovanni was still alive and approaching him fast with a machete, and with one swing he decapitated Carlos' hand which headed to the floor still holding the stake. Turning towards Giovanni, Carlos ducked down preventing another swing from narrowly missing his head, and instead of firing his silver dust bullet at Drago, Carlos had no choice but fire it at Giovanni that let out a small groan as he fell atop his downed master who was still convulsing in pain; Giovanni then shuddered into stillness. Full of rage Carlos fired and almost emptied his gun into them both, screaming out in agonizing pain.

"Good the evil is dead, how easy it was this time."

At that moment a man burst into the warehouse with his crew, just after the first wave of attack, he was surrounded by mercenaries that kept him close, shielding him as if he were the president. It was only the severity of the stifling fetid smell, that struck him hard, causing him to stop for a second and attempt to swallow down the need to vomit. Quickly gathering himself, he glanced at his tracking monitor and pointed the directed to his protection squad. After spotting the syringe like dart, that previously dropped to the floor from Drago's neck, he made a beeline for it and thankfully noticed it hadn't been damaged during the gunfire and chaos. But, in his haste to retrieve it he tripped, and face planted on the uneven dusty floor. With his nose now broken, he managed to grab the dart, then clumsily placed it into a small, padded container, while staggering to his feet. He briefly stared at Carlos, then turned and dashed towards the exit smirking while being followed with stunned looks, and then he was gone.

After the penny dropped Carlos became incandescent with rage, yelling after him.

"What the...you weren't supposed to be here...damn me for a fool, it was the blood you were after all along. I will kill you when I find you, you two faced bastard."

But the man was long gone as his surviving mercenaries peeled off after him, leaving Carlos to fathom the consequences with his own men that were still engaged in heavy fighting on the warehouse floor.

Brody, with eyes almost bulging out of his head, let out a desperate muffled scream on wanting to be released, it intensified with the dart still protruding from the top of his head, but all Carlos said was...

"You are excess to requirements, there are to be no witnesses."

He fired at the now hysterical Brody, with the exploding bullet splitting the top part of his head in two, like the parting of the red sea, it instantly killed him. Brain matter and blood splattered everywhere, especially over Lilly who cringed with the impact. She frantically looked around for a means of escape, but nothing could help, so slid down upon the commode like a spoilt child as desperation gripped at her, for all she could do was await the outcome of her fate. Looking over at Brody, she realised she was on her own, he was no use to anyone anymore, the disgust she had felt towards him was immense, and she would have killed him herself given half the chance, but still, that was a sorry way to die at the hand of an associate.

Carlos turned awkwardly towards Lilly, squeezing his bleeding stump under the armpit of his gun arm which was pointing in her direction; she flinched for there was nothing else she could do. Carlos so wanted to punch the air in victory, because he genuinely thought he had won, but all he got was a slap in the face from defeat. For just as he was about to pull the trigger on her, Drago made a last-ditch effort to turn the tables on him by managing to push Giovanni's limp body aside, and even in his weakened state, with the last of his strength, Drago shoved Carlos onto Lilly as he yelled out.

"Bite him, KILL HIM.'

In that moment of no return, she had no choice but sink her teeth into Carlos' neck. The euphoria of tasting his blood was instant, it engulfed her, while she savagely drained him into weakness as his wriggling became slower. It filled her mouth with ecstasy, her tongue felt like it was full of electrical pulses jolting her with energy. Yet, a small part of Lilly knew what she was doing was horribly wrong, even evil, but that bout of empathy was quickly squashed by the need to survive. Soon she didn't care as the feeling was like an aphrodisiac, she was aroused to the extreme and it was the most incredible sensation she had ever felt.

Drago crept slowly towards her, as if he were crawling under barbed wire, and reached out with a sharp fingernail slicing at Lilly's restraints. They looked at each other, more like glanced, as she twisted and turned herself free for an escape. Not done yet, Drago rolled onto the now collapsed Carlos, then bit and drank the blood still pumping out of the open wound of his stump, he desperately needed fresh blood to eradicate the effect of the silver liquid.

Now free and with all her senses heightened she saw Carlos' snipers skulk into the dimly lit room. Shots were fired at her and the remaining underlings, who wriggled like worms on a hook before collapsing to the ground in blooded heaps. Miraculously none hit her as she pounced on one, slamming him to the ground, then stamped on his head to watch in fascination as it split like a ripened watermelon. The other sniper didn't stand a chance either, he didn't even have time to point his rifle for she moved fast, faster than she had ever moved before and buried her teeth into his neck to drink the vitalising blood.

Lilly's alertness was catapulted by her newly found energy drink, finding herself on a war footing, probably able to take down a handful of men all at once. She could feel her own blood coursing through her veins, caressing and fixing her wounds, it was exhilarating. How deliciously addictive it had become in such a short space of time; the sweet intoxicating blood had bolstered her to a higher plain. It seemed a monster had weld up from within her very soul, and like a battering ram forced its way forward, attempting to trample over every sweet emotion she had ever held dear. Lilly knew she had to take control of herself fast, for the beast had lay dormant deep inside her inner self for so long and was now on the rampage. She remembered Drago's words of bloodlust consuming newbie vampires, *'But I'm not a whole monster, only half,'* her thoughts jostled for an explanation. Fear grasped at her throat, she panicked and struggled to breath, so turned and looked in Drago's direction for words of advice, but he had gone, and so astonishingly had Carlos.

She found herself alone, surrounded by corpses, and her newly manifested mental torment.

***

As Lilly stood on shaky legs, she stared at her surroundings and struggled to take in all that had happened with the utter carnage that spread across the warehouse. It was akin to something out of a horror movie, no more like a war film, for even an RPG had been used to blast their way in, adding fear to the element of surprise. Blood, brain matter and body parts were strewn from the office, out onto the zigzagging staircase, with the discarded bodies of underlings and mercenaries scattered amongst the dusty boxes of rubbish. The scurrying rats had hesitantly returned and began their feast.

She was shaking, it was the shock kicking into her system, *'Jeez,'* she thought, *'a full fat can of cola wouldn't go a miss.'* The first horror that caught her eye was the pitiful sight of Giovanni, obviously dead yet still clutching the contents of his stomach which had been blasted out of him. His intestines were entwined through his fingers, and what she presumed was his bowls or stomach were covering his lap, his face was frozen in an image of pure fear and terror. Her eyes were then drawn to Brody who was still slumped on the commode, the detachable basin had come loose with foulness seeping out, but now half his head was missing due to the exploding tipped bullet being fired into it, silver dust glistened along the edges. Lilly was covered in his blood and brain matter; she was having to concentrate on not vomiting everywhere. Skidding slightly on the disgusting mess that littered the entire room, she cast a look in the direction to where she had last seen Carlos lying in a pool of blood. *'Where was he? Surely, he couldn't have survived the attack with his injuries. How did he manage to escape? Or did Drago drag him away somehow?'* she puzzled.

Carlos not only had his hand chopped off, but had also been bitten by both her and Drago, *'Did I really do that?'* She just couldn't believe she had actually sunk her teeth into another human being, where she had not only bitten but also sucked out blood too. Feeling ashamed over what she had done, and it wasn't just him, for the man dressed in black over there was one of the snipers that crept into the room checking for Carlos, he too was a victim of her bite. Shuddering with the disgust that flowed through her, she held her blood covered head in her hands and moaned to herself.

"No, no, no this can't be happening, what the fuck, what the fuck have I done, I just want to go home."

Suddenly an overwhelming urge to vomit surged through her, she swung around and emptied the contents of her stomach all over Giovanni and now her sick was mingled with intestinal mess and gore. She had to get out of there and fast, as being on her own couldn't be any more depressing or scarier. Nobody was going to rescue her, but somehow, she had to get herself back to the hotel and then to the airport. All she wanted was to get back to New York, and into the safe arms of her father.

A dripping tap over in one of the corners of the warehouse prompted her over, to attempt washing the fast-congealing blood off, so not to draw too much attention to herself. But she had to act fast as the police sirens were getting speedily closer.

***

How she made it back to her hotel from the horrors of the warehouse, that was in the Secondigliano district, she will never know. She ran constantly at the speed of a world class sprinter, avoiding people skilfully like the scooters that barely miss pedestrians walking along the narrow streets. It was a complete blur, seeming like she had ran through a hazy fog, where faces looked at her then turned away, not wanting to get involved as they tried to focus their shocked stares elsewhere.

Finally, on arriving at her hotel, she bypassed the elevator and ran up the stairs, stumbled along the corridor, and how she got to her room unseen was an utter miracle. After securely locking herself in, even dragging furniture across to barricade the door, she collapsed onto the bedroom floor panting and attempting to get her breath back. She eventually picked herself up and stood in front of the bedroom mirror, *'What the actual fuck has happened, this has to be a nightmare, this can't be real, can it? I am not Lillith the killer dhampir, I am just plain Lilly from New York, I'm not a blood sucking monster.'* She studied her face looking for any changes to her appearance, was her skin a different tone, had her mouth changed shape? No, there was nothing different about her at all, yet when she looked deeply at her reflection, she could see a difference, it was subtle. She noticed that her eyes were a deeper shade of red, and her skin although filthy and grimy seemed to glow underneath, *'well at least I still have a reflection, that must mean I'm not like him, doesn't it?'*

Lilly stripped off, dumping her clothes into a pile, and took a good look at her nakedness in the bathroom mirror.

Was it her imagination or did she look more muscular and leaner, *'Fuck me, I look fantastic!'* The bruises, of which she was sure, that once covered her body were now gone, including the cuts and scrapes she received in the battle, all had also disappeared. Amazingly her skin was smooth and injury free, this is what started to freak her out, *'Have I turned into a superhuman type monster, what the actual hell has happened to me?'* She ran a steaming hot shower, and as the water began running red from the blood that was in her hair, Lilly felt bits of goodness knows what falling out, and just assumed it was brains and guts that had got entangled into it. She shampooed it twice, no three times, to make sure it was finally rid of anything disgusting. The relaxing scent of the lavender and chamomile shower gel was rubbed vigorously, by way of a flannel, into her pores in a desperate attempt at ridding the scent of death that had permeated from her. Soon a tidal wave of emotions hit Lilly all at once, it was almost powerful as the spray from the showerhead above her, and she sunk to the floor hugging her knees to her chest, rocking herself back and forth sobbing like a baby *'I just want to go home.'* she repeated to herself over and over again. Thousands of thoughts screamed through her mind, she couldn't begin to comprehend what she had just experienced, *'Jesus, I am going to need so much therapy when I get out of here.'* The mere thought of her biological father being a vampire was too much for Lilly to process, *'it can't be true, there had to be some mistake'*. The monster who was allegedly her parent had left her there alone, in that horrific place of destruction and chaos. For if he was indeed her father then surely he would have taken her with him to safety, and not left her there to fend for herself.

Lilly crawled into bed and gathered the sheets around herself, as if in a protective cocoon, sleep would more than likely sidestep her exhaustion, she wasn't even sure if she would ever sleep again.

The airport
Chapter 9

VERY EARLY THE next morning, after a fitful night's sleep, Lilly had woken with a start accompanied by the worst headache imaginable. She found herself punching the air in a violent tussle, after finding herself tangled up in the bed covers, shivering with goose bumps and in a cold sweat. Her head thumped painfully with an intense penetrating pulse, causing her to stumble into the bathroom and flip over her wash bag in a desperate effort at finding paracetamols amongst the mess. There were four left in the blister pack as she thumbed them through and washed them down with what was left in a small vodka bottle, she strangely found amongst the others scattered by the basin. *'What the fuck did I do last night?'* She had previously lost her sense of care before crashing out after raiding the now empty minibar, in a dismal attempt at easing the twisted thoughts that swirled and tormented her thoughts. To think that alcohol could help was foolish after witnessing and experiencing what she had done. Yet, for the briefest of moments it did, by eradicating the horror that was polluting her mind and even as she blacked out previously, deep down she knew it would be forever impossible.

After catching a few hours' sleep, her tormented dreams began to surface. Firstly, the beauty of Pompei drifted into her subconscious state with all its history and architecture, and while exploring she somehow managed to lose her tour guide, a very annoying man with flapping arms who constantly asked 'Do you know what this is? Do you know what they used this for?' 'No, I don't bloody know, that's why you're the guide and I'm the tourist, so just tell me what the fuck it is,' she screamed at him in her dream like state. Soon finding herself alone enjoying the solitude, photographing the murals and artefacts to sketch later, when suddenly her dream got darker and was interrupted with the image of Brody tied to a chair placed in the centre of one of the villas. His eyes had been gouged out, his nose and ears sliced off and standing behind him was a tall dark menacing figure who Lilly couldn't quite see yet strangely knew who it was. A hand then reached round, grabbing Brody's head in a vice-like grip, and before she could stop what was about to happen it was snapped back with tremendous force, to then have the face of Drago abruptly appear with fangs bared. He sank them deep into the Brody's neck, sucking ferociously on his blood, draining him, leaving Lilly petrified and unable to move as she seemed stuck to the spot. She tried opening her mouth to scream but just couldn't, no matter how hard she tried, not a sound escaped her lips. He quickly swayed aside, like something out of the Matrix, where Drago narrowly avoided the bullet blasted out of Carlos' gun which hit and split Brody's head wide open instead, leaving Drago sneering at her for some weird reason. Blood dripped from his fangs as he beckoned her over to join him, his mouth wasn't moving yet she could hear him speak to her, [Come Lillith, come join me in the feast] this time she could move, so turned and ran as fast as she could, stumbling over decapitated bodies covering the large cobble stones of the streets, tripping over them in haste, trying desperately to get away from the horror she had witnessed. Her legs pumping faster than ever before, with a running track along the centre of the street, as escaping from there and getting to safety was all she wanted. Yet every turn she took she found herself back in the same villa, the same from where she began, and the frustration gripped at her. It became a maze of streets which she couldn't escape from, and Brody was always there, looking to her for help, the help she could never give.

Now in the bathroom she turned sharply and only just made to the toilet bowl, then began puking her guts up from all the alcohol she had drunk earlier. She couldn't stop her body from shaking, with the sweat and smell of rottenness still seeping out of her pores, '*Jesus, I am rank, I stink*', she thought. Having very little choice, she picked out the paracetamols from the sick and re-swallowed them, she was in right old state. Peering at herself in the mirror, she grew angry over becoming accustomed to what was now reflected back, and the intensity of her anger made her fear the outcome of what she could potentially deliver to others. The resentment she felt was all consuming, as her reflection began to display the hollow look of despair, she was emotionally exhausted. So, in an attempt to rid herself of the scent of death Lilly had a shower, where she frantically scrubbed her body all over, then grabbed some clean clothes while she checked her watch. It was still only 3.30 am and she had time to get to the airport before her flight. Thankfully, she had managed to get a seat on the first flight out of Naples back to New York. It cost her, but she didn't care as the 6 am departure could not come sooner. Even the thought of a twelve-hour flight was soothing as it might help her try and gather herself in an attempt of beginning to process what she had been through, before she met her father James again.

How on earth was she ever going to explain what had happened to her, hell, she couldn't even explain it to herself. Where would she start *"Hey dad, you will never guess what happened to me in Naples, I met my real dad and you will never believe it, but he is a fucking vampire called Drago aka Dracula."* She threw all her clothes and toiletries into her rucksack, grabbed her handbag, then left the room. As it was still early, she managed to avoid seeing the hotel receptionists who must have been getting their first coffee of the day in the back room of the reception area, so left without checking out, '*just add that to my list of crimes*' she mulled to herself.

On arrival at the airport, Lilly got out of the taxi quick time, threw a handful of Euros at the driver whose face suddenly lit up, then made her way to the already busy entrance. Several clouds of smoke wafted across her from all the cigarettes and vapes that people were desperately puffing on, passengers grabbing their one last hit of nicotine before they entered the building to catch their flights and be dispersed across the globe. For a moment

Lilly thought of trying one herself, to see if it might calm her nerves, but the smell and nausea which crept through her swiftly change her mind.

Only having her rucksack and handbag, Lilly realised she had no need to go through the check in process, so began wandering around the airport before she had to make her way through security. The thought of passing the security gate keepers was making her agitated and nervous, almost paranoid. Were the authorities already looking for her, waiting for her to appear, watching her movements, ready to pounce and handcuff her? *'Surely the place should be swarming with the police, shouldn't it?' It would have made the news by now, yes? All that noise from the gun fire must have been heard from miles away. All the bodies, someone would have discovered them and raised the alarm. My DNA would be all over the place?'* As she walked, she felt as if she was on a highwire, trying to keep herself from falling into to the abyss of madness, desperately struggling to keep her mind in balance. She had to keep a check on herself, *'just keep your shit together baby'*.

The restaurants and cafes were opening for the day, but the thought of eating anything was too much, her stomach was in knots and she was sure of just vomit anything back up. The strong smell of the coffee brewing was nauseating to her, yet on any other occasion she would love to have a strong espresso to perk her up for the day, but today was no normal day, *'I left America an innocent woman and returning a blood thirsty killer'* she gloomily mused.

Amongst the queue going through security, her nerves and senses were on high alert. She could hear the conversations going on all around her, buzzing in her mind like a thousand annoying flies. It transported her back to High School where she had learnt on how to zone them out and concentrate on what she had to do. *'Focus, focus, focus.'* She was aware of herself sweating and trembling, so really had to get a grip before going through security, without being noticed. *'Just take deep breaths,'* she repeated to herself as she fumbled taking off her jacket. The sweat patches under her armpits were spreading, and she tried to keep her hands from shaking while placing her bag and rucksack into the grey tray, THEN watched it go through the scanner, praying that nothing would be flagged up. She was summoned forward by a stern looking security guard, and on trembling legs Lilly made her way towards the body scanner, it seemed to be the slowest walk she had ever taken, almost forgetting how to put one foot in front of the other.

Paranoia took hold, and her thoughts drifted, she was convinced on somehow being different after tasting blood for the first time, *'damn it, I've actually bitten someone, would my body look different on the inside,'* she knew this was ludicrous, but her paranoia had hit level code red. It was as if time stood still while waiting for the nod to continue through the machine, and when she got it, Lilly could have wept with relief when not stopped. Grabbing at her jacket and bags, she had to restrain herself from running to the nearest toilet to be sick again.

Waiting in the toilet queue, trying not to vomit, she was shoved in the back by a clumsy woman's large handbag which was clearly an accident, but Lilly spun around in an instant, ready to explode with her nerves on edge, and almost grabbed the woman ready to slam her into a wall. She had to show great self-restraint and will power in not reacting that way, then she caught sight of her reflection in the bathroom mirror, she almost looked unrecognisable to herself. Her face was distorted with rage, her eyes were blazing red, and she had a strong desire to bite into the woman's neck and taste her blood. She shoved the innocent woman roughly away from her, then barged her way into a now emptying cubicle. Inside Lilly sat and attempted to control her urge to taste blood again, the desire was growing stronger, *"Just one more taste that's all I need. Stop it, what the fuck is happening to me, deep breaths Lilly, come on hold it together girl, you are nearly home, oh come on just one more taste, NO, just stop it, stop it, stop it,"* she sternly thought, *"is this how the people outside smoking feel, am I addicted to blood now, I know it's so wrong on every level of humanity, but Goodness knows I am craving the taste, what the actual fuck, someone, anybody, please help me."* Lilly knew she had to pull herself together, so not to draw attention to herself. The poor innocent woman Lilly had shoved was still in the bathroom when Lilly came out of the toilet.

"I am so sorry ma'am, I don't know what came over me, all I can put it down to is my nerves. I really hate flying, I have a fear of it, I am so sorry, I really didn't mean to shove you like that, I don't realise my own strength at times."

Knowing she was waffling, Lilly had to get out of the bathroom quickly, before the woman drew attention by complaining, and before anyone became suspicious of her. Thankfully the woman appeared not to understand a single word being said but cautiously leaned away while giving Lilly a really filthy look, shrugged her shoulders and turned to continue applying lipstick.

After finding which departure gate to head for, Lilly was still looking all around and checking for anyone who might seem suspicious, an odd movement or stare would be enough for her to stampede for the boarding queue. She honestly wouldn't feel safe until she was back in New York, and even then, might panic at border control. *'Just keep your shit together woman,'* she anguished, half convinced that at any moment someone was going to grab her by the arm and request she come with them for questioning. Like an enormous red arrow was floating above her head, saying 'Here I am, come and get me'. Now, desperately trying not to make eye contact with anyone, being conscious of not looking guilty over having something terrible to hide, which in fact was being a murderer, or even worse, a blood thirsty monster who took enjoyment from drinking another human's blood. Could it get any more disgusting to her, killing in cold blood, *'What have I become, this can't be real, this only happens in the movies not to a normal girl like me?'* Yet, knowing she could never be that 'normal' girl again crushed her very soul while waiting to board her flight. She was deeply sad, and started to wish she could turn back time and erase the last few months, from discovering the DNA test results, to meeting that despicable piece of shit Brody and the nightmare that was soon to engulf her. The sights she had witnessed would be forever imprinted in her mind, how could she ever erase them from her dreams or even reality. The knowledge which had been given to her by what she now knew to sadly be her biological father, was something she had never wished for, or wanted to believe. The evilness she had witnessed in that place was all too true, she had been there, she had seen it all happen, and for the sake of saving her own life, had taken part in it too, making her an accomplice to murder. The feelings of utter panic, fear and paranoia swept over her again as her whole body seemed to shudder. She tried desperately to remember her calm breathing exercises in an attempt to achieve some sort of normality, it wasn't working.

Suddenly, to her horror, *'Holy shit, no, no, no…'* Lilly began to feel that now recognisable intrusive vibrating sensation which sent shivers tingling down her spine, it was the same foreboding feeling of when she had first encountered Drago.

[Is it you, you monster? But it's daylight, don't your lot burn in sunlight]

She sent out telepathically, not wanting, but strangely wanting a reply, but all she noticed was a fat bald man jump up and look around in a fit of confusion, *'Oh shit,'* Lilly thought, *'I've got to focus more, and avoid mind talking to the wrong person.'* The man continued to look baffled, scratching a reddening patch on his head, then sat down and sporadically looked around in bewilderment.

For the first time since the horror began a smile crept across her face, it was just the reaction from the bald man which was amusing and, at that moment, priceless. The vibrations began again.

[You're alive aren't you]

She tried again, knowing Drago was close, but she couldn't see him anywhere. Once, she would have logically thought of not seeing him during the daylight, but she remembered Drago saying something about things not being as they are in the movies. Desperately looking around, whipping her head this way and that, she sent out more telepathic connections, but this time carefully avoiding others, especially the bald man who was still ever so slightly bemused.

[Bloody show yourself] Lilly complained with mounting annoyance.

Her frustration grew, feeling like a cyclist ferociously peddling and getting nowhere, as she continued to nervously look around, desperately trying to see him for she knew he was there, but where? She understood that he is a master of deception, and has had years to perfect his craft, to only make himself known if he so wished. Soon, the soft sound of a seductive whisper came across, it was somewhat sad, yet still sinister as it edged its way further into her mind.

[You are leaving me so soon dear Lillith]

[I knew you were here, hah, where are you? Will you not burn from the sunlight, as you should you monster,]

Was all she could say as her anger increased, but she was also totally overcome with her feelings of longing, even her absurd feeling of love for him, such as an abused partner longs for the wanting of their abuser.

[well]

[Burning to a cinder is for the movies, we feel the sun, it is hot and extremely uncomfortable, that is all] came the reply.

[Where are you?] she hesitantly asked.

[Never you mind. Have you healed?]

[Why do you even care you monster, you left me alone high and dry to fend for myself, why am I even conversing with you]

[Because you are drawn to me dear Lillith]

Her anger rose for he was right, and she hated herself even more for it.

[Why aren't the police all over this? It was like a war zone, how are they not here after me...]

[Shhhhh, don't bother yourself, it has all been taken care of. That's why I had to leave so quickly, to contain collateral damage as such, I know many within the authorities and strings had to be pulled fast. The explosion announced the arrival of terror and drew attention from the city, something that I have avoided for centuries. Acts of terrorism from certain factions has always been used to cover misdoings, it plays well with the public at large. Gang violence often covers vampire attacks. It has all been covered dear Lillith, you are safe]

[Safe, safe you say, what has happened to me, my mind is about to explode]

[All I can advise is for you to gather yourself, be strong, and all this confusion shall pass]

She could still sense, almost taste his pure evilness, but there was the undertone of sadness wrapped around his words. Still, the hairs on the back of her neck were standing up and she felt a similar feeling of evil welling within her soul, combined with the panic and fear which began to engulf her, feeling as if she were about to explode with confusion.

[But…but what shall I do? What will you do? I…you...what…]

[What you do from now on is your choice, as for me I am at a loss dear Lillith. I have lost my faithful Giovani, someone I loved very deeply, in my own way, but I need to gather my strength once more, as I have done many times in the past. We will meet again my daughter]

"NO…NO, DON'T GO, DON'T LEAVE ME," she shouted for all around her to hear, but was only met with worried strange looks, and agonising silence from within her mind.

Almost, and for good reason, anger began pulsing through her body again, even worse this time. Blood lust raced inside of her, with a strong desire to bite the judgemental man sitting opposite and nearly took her over. *'Don't fucking look at me like that, I could rip you apart before a single shot is fired by the police over there,'* she angrily thought. To taste and watch his pain, to sense his shock as her teeth sank into his flesh, *'bite him, bite him, it is your destiny girl.'* Lilly's evil side whispered from within.

It was a desire so strong she felt it straining to overtake her sense of control, looking around all she could see were bright colours everywhere bouncing off the walls and the windows, her hearing was heightened as if she could hear all conversations, with the different scents and smells coming from people which was so intoxicating. She wanted to taste their blood, drink from them, it was as if she had become a crack addict and was seeking the next high, to see if it would match the first. *'Get a fucking grip of yourself woman,'* she angrily told herself, then took a very deep breath, held it for as long as she could, then breathed out, soon her breathing regulated as did her self-control.

Conscious of not drawing any further attention to herself, Lilly took a book out of her bag, it was a reference book about the museums and galleries in Naples, with places she had sadly not been able to visit and admire. She was regretful that she hadn't got to see the beauty and magnificence of the Veiled Christ for herself. It was something she had wanted to see for so long, and the only description she had was from Drago, his description being so beautiful warm and tender, two words she could never quite place in the same sentence with him. Lilly was aware she wasn't reading any of the words in front of her, they were all just a blur as her eyes filled with tears, she was trying so hard not to cry and draw any more unnecessary attention to herself. Holding the book to her face was just an attempt in keeping people from noticing her mini meltdown, and had to somehow calm herself. Knowing she wasn't a bad or evil person, yet the thoughts and desires that were coursing through her veins were truly petrifying. She was horrified, no terrified with the thought of longing to encounter Drago again. However, she was mercifully aware that he would have to keep a very low profile for many years to come after what had happened in the warehouse, which was a comfort to her more sensible side.

Yet, the anger and rage Lilly felt welling up inside her towards Drago was understandably overwhelming, how dare that monster completely upend her life. She was just an average New Yorker living her best life, every day was more or less the same, home, work, out with friends, spending time with her dad, then BOOM, it all changed. Everything she had ever held dear was in fact a lie, her whole life and existence was a lie. The anger was bubbling inside her threatening to erupt at any moment again, like the volcano Vesuvius she could see out of the aeroplane window during take-off. She could feel the adrenaline pumping through her veins, how was she ever going to recover from this trauma and experience. Who would believe her even if she attempted to explain it, no one in their right mind would. She was allegedly a dhampir, that's what Drago had reluctantly called her, and until yesterday she had never heard of the word. She was one, a freak of nature, a monster, what was she supposed to do with this mind-blowing information. She tried to calm herself in the confined claustrophobic space of the plane seat by tapping each side of her forehead temples, it was a trick she was taught years ago whilst at High School. A school councillor had shown her the effectiveness of mindfulness, but today it wasn't working, she didn't think anything would ever work again. How could her life ever go back to some form of normality, after the destruction of life and evilness she had witnessed in what she had thought was such a beautiful part of the world, where her mother's family was from.

Lilly began scrolling through her phone, she went through all the photos taken before the nightmare had begun. Photos of the narrow streets, the restaurants, shops and cafes, she could almost smell the aroma, even taste the food being cooked, the garlic and fresh herbs, and the sweetness of the freshly cooked pastries. Even the fresh smell of the washing constantly hanging from the windows of the houses, the often-felt dripping water coming from the clothes. She could hear the continuous sounds of the beeping of horns coming from cars, but mostly scooters, with the buzz and the feeling of excitement coming out through her phone screen. Naples was vibrant and intoxicating, but also dirty and gritty, with graffiti written everywhere you looked, with crumbling plaster peeling from walls that were pot marked with decaying age. Yet she now knew there was another side, a dangerous sinister side to Naples which people rarely saw, a side she wished she had never encountered. The only tourist activity she had managed to experience was the day trip to Pompei, with the train journey being itself an interesting event with tourists like herself and Brody crammed in like sardines, ready to explore the streets of Pompeii. She was happy there strolling along, when Lilly discovered a villa named La Casa Deivettii which had a fresco in the doorway of a man with a humongous penis, it was the only time that Brody showed any interest in Pompei, making him even more excited with the other rather rude frescos within the villa walls that depicted sexual positions. She remembered him saying loudly 'Cool, this must have been a whore house', she had been so embarrassed with his ignorance.

Oh, but how she had loved it there, with the tragedy and beauty of Pompeii so hard to put into words. The history of it was all around her, the torment and terror that its inhabitants had endured was hard to imagine. Yet, the breathtaking, no, painstaking restoration of the site was a joy to her, and whilst wandering around she had pictured herself working there, being part of the archaeology team, spending days in the sun methodically scrapping away with a small trowel and brush to unearth its treasures and secrets. She imagined finding stunning frescos that had been hidden away for centuries, the colours still vibrant and clear, coming across pieces of jewellery that had been worn by rich ladies, and possibly unearthing a body that had been buried under the ash and rubble perfectly intact. The mental image of a body sadly brought Lilly back to the present moment, and distress, where fear and panic washed over her again. How could she have been so gullible and naïve, her 'shit-o-meter' must have run out of batteries when it came to meeting the arsehole Brody. She began to question it all, everything had been an elaborate plan to trick and lie to her, she was so angry with herself for falling for it all. *'Where were my super fucking senses then?'* Why had she not picked up on the bullshit lies he spewed at her, the way he acted like the perfect gentleman, paying for everything; had she been that desperate and vulnerable to have fallen for it all. His handsomeness and charm had sucked her in, just as he had planned. Well, he certainly wouldn't be playing his charming tricks anymore, especially with half of his head blown off, she hoped he rot in hell for what he had put her through and was slightly shocked at herself for feeling so uncaring and dismissive of his demise. But then she sharply reminded herself he was a shit bag liar, and most of all a coward who was just out for himself.

Sadly, it made Lilly question if she would ever be able to trust any man ever again, were they all liars? Even her dad had lied to her. For all her life she had only known him to be her father, and now she knew for certain it was another made up story. She understood it was to protect the memory of her mother and her relationship with James, but the truth was unimaginable and horrific, *'My birth father is a fucking vampire'*. It blew her mind.

Lilly was struggling with trying to put all the pieces together, with what had taken place. One minute she and Brody had been tied up in chairs, then the next men dressed in black with balaclavas burst into the place with explosives and guns. *'Who were they? Were they there to only capture or kill Drago? Was Carlos evil like Drago, but slightly different? And who was the man I had bitten, the men I killed, who were they? Did they have families?'* she depressingly thought. Yet, through the carnage, she was certain about spotting another man there, surrounded by even bigger men in black. He had a bleeding nose, and snatch up something from the floor? It was all too much for Lilly, there were too many questions racing through her mind which needed answers, that might never come. At least trying to sleep might somehow calm herself from the thoughts gone into overdrive, so she beckoned one of the air stewards and asked for something to drink, anything alcoholic that could help her mind slow down. She was only one hour into her twelve-hour flight, and she knew that this was going to be the longest journey home ever, so any relief was gladly welcomed.

On finishing her first drink, that didn't touch the sides, she relaxed but was soon visited by the words that Drago had said, 'This is your new reality dear Lillith, Vlad Dracula's blood is in your veins, it is your destiny, you are my child, a rare child of a human and a vampire. Many will look for you.' She shook her head, trying to rid her mind of his words, so began repeating to herself over and over again, *'No, I am just Lilly from New York, just plain ol' Lilly.'*

***

After finishing her second double whisky, Lilly was restlessly struggling to snuggle down in the vein attempt of getting some sleep, totally oblivious that 3000 miles away on the west coast of America, the man with the bloody nose she had previously spotted during the attack, had already landed and was speedily making his way to the mansion of a dying ruthless multi-billionaire….

The man and the Billionaire
Chapter 10

ALMOST LEAPING DOWN the steps of the private jet plane, a Bombardier Global 8000, he adjusted his aviator sunglasses to conceal two black eyes on receiving a broken nose after tripping over bloodied body parts that were strewn across a virtual war zone. He had face planted the dirty warehouse floor hard, but that was no never mind, for he had achieved the aim of his mission in obtaining what his employer desperately needed, the blood of a Vampire.

His nose throbbed the entire flight, even after receiving gentle administrations of first aid from the rather attractive flight attendant, who had the hands of an angel and the body of a stripper. If it wasn't for the urgency of his mission, and the fact he was exhausted, he might have attempted at having her in the bathroom as he was a fan of the mile high club, with or without her permission. However, he had more important things to be concerned about, with the precious item securely kept inside a padded container which was attached to his wrist via a security chain, such was its value.

There was a pristine white Rolls Royce on the tarmac waiting, engine soundlessly running with the air con set to a comfortable 17 degrees, to speedily escort him to an ailing, dying, unscrupulous Billionaire, who only had days to live. They had both worked together over many years, he being the right-hand man who always got jobs done quickly and efficiently. More often than not, the jobs were mostly on the side of illegality, wiping out whole villages in the pursuit of diamonds, supplying weapons to any murderous regimes that were willing to pay, but was mainly a big player in the narcotics world. The billionaire had a finger on every pulse, only his pulse was dying. These two were no angels, only demons of self-satisfying greed and accumulation.

Sitting comfortably on the fine, natural grain leather seat, he recalled the meeting, where he was tasked a specific mission on finding the impossible elixir of life, virtually anything that would help the billionaire live for longer, at any cost. Initially, he was stunned on being asked to do something which seemed insane as this, but after being sanctioned, the race against time began where he was given carte blanche on money and facilities to be used any which way he wanted. The man just had to find something, anything, because this billionaire didn't want to die from the predicted torturous death that lay ahead of him, he wanted to live, forever if he could. So, through his web of networks, he began to source what he was after, eventually discovering a potential solution that was so outrageous and pathetic to the normal mind. For even to consider it meant you were possibly deranged, and the limited few he began talking to mentioned it was practically futile to achieve. He eventually discovered a man in New York, after torturing the information out of the limited few, and found what was supposedly the 'expert'. But, on investigation, this so-called extraordinarily rare expert was the shell of the man he once was, a broken man in every way or sense of the word, who voluntarily resided in a mental institution. He wouldn't cooperate in the slightest, refusing point blank, saying it was far too dangerous. Even when he was offered vast amounts of money he still refused, and threating the death or kidnapping of loved ones, to then be cut into pieces if he didn't comply, wouldn't make him reconsider as he had no one left, they were already dead; for the things he had once hunted had already taken severe retribution on him. But he did drop a name, the name of Carlos in Argentina, he was almost all that was left of what he was looking for. After finding this Carlos, he got all the information he needed and used him purely as a means to an end. He fooled Carlos into believing he was a trophy hunter, a big game hunter and the prize he craved was something unbelievable to most, and travelled the world seeking out someone that could help him in his quest. What he wanted was a live vampire, but deceivingly said it was only for its head, and that he alone wanted to kill it. But it was wanted for another reason, he wanted its blood as he erroneously thought it could hold the elixir of life, something the billionaire desperately sought after. So basically, he double crossed Carlos to receive the vampire blood.

***

"Welcome back Mr Venator, the Vip (Very important person, meaning the Boss) has been waiting for you," said a massive bodyguard standing by the gates of an incredible mansion which lay ahead, "you can proceed."

He nodded to the driver who accelerated along the gravelled driveway, then eventually skidded with a sliding crunching sound, speed was of the essence as the Vip was waiting.

Mr Venator was met by yet another massive bodyguard who quietly, so as not to disturb its occupier, escorted him to a huge opulently decorated room which had floor to ceiling heavy drapes pulled aside to allow for the first rays of sunrise to enter. The artwork hanging on the walls were stunning masterpieces by Monet, Vincent van Gogh and Renoir, he found himself having to drag his eyes away from the beauty of them all, to focus on what was in the centre of this art gallery. The bodyguard ushered him forward where a nurse approached and told Mr Venator to put on sterilised gloves, including mask, then beckoned him to a translucent germ-free environment, where she pulled aside an opening and pointed at a spot for him to wait. He looked inside another screened off sterile bubble, and saw a large bed covered in fur throws, soft silk sheets in muted shades of grey, with several propped up pillows upon which lay the sight of a frail looking man who had demanded and bankrolled this entire desperate assignment. There was yet another nurse inside wearing complete sterile clothing, who looked up for a second, then continued checking the monitors displaying vital signs, with the constant low-level hum and whooshing sound that indicated the delivery of oxygen.

The rising sun pierced through the sparce flakes of floating dust, that gave their germophobe Vip an ethereal appearance, as if he had a halo above his head. One could tell he had not long to live, as he the stench of impending death seemed to permeate the room, a cloying sickly scent that stuck to the back of one's throat which Mr Venator was familiar with.

With a liver spotted quivering hand the Vip flicked it at the nurse, a signal for her to leave, then lifted the oxygen mask from his face, and with a raspy voice asked in the steely determination of a dying man, that didn't want to die.

"Well? Do you have it?"

"Yes sir." Mr Venator answered.

"So, this vampire, what was he like?"

"How can I describe the horror I witnessed."

"I don't care about the horror, just tell me about him."

"Sir, he was incredible, for even in his weakened state after the silver liquid hit him, he was more powerful than you could ever imagine."

"Hmmm, I see." a slight smile crept along the Vip's face.

"And as you requested sir, all mercenaries, including myself wore body cameras. Would you like me to connect and show you?"

"No, just show me the blood."

Mr Venator lifted the briefcase like container and opened it, spine in towards himself and displayed the contents.

"Bring it to me." came a rasping order.

"What? But your sterile environment sir. Do you not wish to get it checked first? At least let me…"

"Damn it man, I don't have time. None of us gets out of this alive, we're all virtually dead already, it's just that we don't know when we'll punch out on the clock of life, and I don't want to die, so just fucking bring it to me."

Mr Venator approached through the protective screen, looked at the startled nurse, then placed the case beside the Vip.

"Is that it?" questioned the Vip, surprised on how unimpressive it looked.

"Why yes sir, this is the true blood of a vampire, and not just any vampire. If you ever thought the theme of Dracula was a total work of fiction, then think again. This blood came from Dracula himself."

The Vip and the eavesdropping nurse were stunned.

"Are you telling me…"

The Vip didn't finish the question, as the startling made him feel even weaker.

"Yes sir, it's all true. I saw him with my own eyes."

"Tell me more about this…this Dracula." the Vip rasped the question after gathering himself.

"He was, in my expert opinion, the most dangerous thing I had ever come across in my life. I like to think that I'm a hard man, and I have witnessed the most horrendous of killings, but what I witnessed in that warehouse was truly the most terrifying of them all. To see what I had seen, an actual vampire ripping another man's throat out with his teeth and drinking the blood, tearing arms off with his bare hands, ripping off a head then stamping on it as if it were a bug. The strength of the monster was incredible, and to be very honest, it was petrifying to see."

"How I would have loved to have seen that," said the Vip drifting into his imagination, then he asked, "is he dead now?"

"Yes, I presume so."

"You presume?"

"Sir, Carlos would have seen to that, not only was he given strict instructions for no other witnesses and believe me in his murderous rage that bastard would have killed everything. I was more concerned with the vampire blood, it was my number one priority, a once in a multigenerational chance, it had to be taken."

"You are right, I'm dancing on a pin head, for the circumstances on how you got it all pales into insignificance. Let us begin, I am the guineapig for this 'experiment', and it is mine alone. We don't even know if it will work, but I will try anything, I want to live."

"Yes, I know, but the chances of this working are negligible sir. Even if it does, which is highly unlikely, think of the consequences of its impact, this is not a temporary change its permanent."

"I know what I am doing and what I need, the permutations have been going through my mind since you suggested this. I have nothing to lose yet everything to gain, and that is my fucking life back. I am not ready to die. I have paid you handsomely, do not forget, so get on with it.'

At that, Mr Venator lifted the syringe like dart out of the briefcase and handed it to the nurse.

"What? No, I can't," the nurse complained, "I must warn you this is highly dangerous, have you really thought all this through thoroughly? Sir, I only have your best interests at heart sir, and this is very irregular. Not to mention this blood could actually hasten your death, not prevent it."

"Listen you stupid bitch," strained the Vip, "I am not paying you to think or have an opinion. If I wasn't so fucking weak, I would do it myself. Yet sadly for me I need your assistance, so if you want your wage and your life just do what you are fucking told to do."

"I must say," the nurse continued to argue, "this goes against my ethical views in every way."

She had been instructed to be with him at all times, on a twelve-hour shift switched with another, and the thought of what was about to happen chilled her to the bone.

"You heard the man, just do what he says and get on with it. Give him what he wants, or I will put a bullet in your head, do you understand me?' the hard voice of Mr Venator spoke into her ear.

It was then that the nurse felt what she presumed was the cold hard steel of a gun pressing into the back of her head. She froze with fear, her hand holding the tube to the canula was shaking and used her other hand to hold it steady. She was petrified, but now knew what she had to do, to live. This was the best paid job she had ever had, helping to pay off the gambling debts of her no-good husband. It even meant she could finally set up a college fund for her daughter, so she had no intention of dying, now having too much to live for, but couldn't help but ask one last time before she released the contents into his veins. She looked down at him and softly said.

"Sir, are ready? If you are, I must ask you one more time, is this really what you want to do, are you sure?"

This was obviously a mentally unstable man dying in his bed, a desperate man who was intent on going through with this madness. He nodded and closed his eyes, so she put her ethical dilemma to one side and reluctantly released the untested blood into the canula. She took a step back and waited, watching the monitor for any changes to the sick man's vitals. Drago's blood entered the Vip's body, and as they looked on with the gun still at the back of the nurse's head, nothing happened, then the sound of the monitor flatlining. Other than that, here was complete silence, until Mr Venator pulled the trigger killing her instantly, her body hitting the floor in a crumpled heap. He called out to a bodyguard who had previously been instructed on what was to happen next.

"Her job was done, and loose ends need to be tied up. Organise a clean-up and get another nurse, then prepare my room, I'm to stay for a few days," he ordered, "oh, and get that unethical nurse back, I don't want to go through this shit again. Get that nurse to stay here at all times, so make up a put you up bed and place it quite close to the Vip. The nurse is to continue monitoring and is strictly forbidden to touch the body. You will watch the body and the nurse from your monitors. Remember, do not touch the body, only observe and monitor for any changes. This might go on for a day, a few days, even a week. Then and only after a week can he be pronounced dead. Contact me instantly if anything happens, do you understand, instantly." he ordered.

The bodyguard nodded, then Mr Venator turned and left the large opulent room.

***

Two days later the same bodyguard urgently called for Mr Venator to come quickly. The sight that greeted him was unadulterated horror, like the ones in Naples. Blood was splattered over the inside of the once sterilised bubble, with bloodied handprints dragged this way and that, blood was everywhere. He then spotted the now dead backup nurse, throat ripped apart, eyes fixed in a stare of death.

"Sweet Jesus, it…it…actually happened. Lock the place down…NOW, DO IT NOW." he screamed at the bodyguard who nervously spoke into his chest two-way radio.

Yes, the nurse was there to monitor the body but was mainly there as a meal if the unthinkable took place. They both rushed to the exit, where suddenly the panicking bodyguard was wrenched upwards almost like a feather, and as the 300lb man hopelessly struggled he kicked outwards hitting Mr Venator in the head, sending him sprawling and landing akimbo on the floor. He tried to rise to his feet but skidded on the dripping blood while desperately trying for the exit. Sheer panic competed with terror as he was intercepted and narrowly missed by the drained bodyguard's corpse hitting the floor in front of him with a bone crunching thud. To his horror he was further blocked from escape, as the nigh impossible had truly happened, and where Mr Venator first looked into the bloodcurdling eyes of pure evil.

Epilogue

TWO YEARS LATER Lilly was sitting on a bench close to a restaurant in Central Park...where she caught a glimpse of a Panama hat which instantly threw her back to the horror she barely survived. It caused her to shiver as the shock of fear gnawed at her again, with her breathing becoming erratic and her heart raced from normal to almost bursting. All her senses sprang to full alert as she spotted the man under that same hat making a beeline for her, who still carried a pronounced limp, it was Carlos. She recognised the smell of his blood, so had no doubt who it was, and held him responsible for the trauma which totally wrecked her life. The last time she saw him was when his hand was freshly cut off, and she had bitten into his neck to prevent him from killing her. It was her first taste of blood which ended up sending her to an addiction clinic on her arrival back in America, but she blamed it on alcohol addiction, obviously. He had a pathetic looking prosthetic hand, that stuck out of his jacket sleeve as if it were from a cheap waxwork museum. *'How the fuck did he survive,'* her stunned thoughts screamed.

He removed his hat and bowed his head to Lilly, he gestured towards the empty place next to her on the bench, then made to sit down.

[What the fuck do you think you are doing] Lilly growled at him telepathically.

Carlos shied away cautiously, for he knew how dangerous she is, and her demeanour showed she was ready to strike.

"Lillith, I come in peace and have approached you in a public place for a reason. You see those police officers over there, they have been instructed by me to shoot you dead if you attack me."

"They wouldn't be able to protect you, you do realise that I could rip your throat out and be gone before they pull their tiggers."

"Yes, maybe so, but you never know, you could be having an off day. I repeat, I come in peace.

"How the hell did you find me? I thought you, no hoped you were dead. Why don't you just fuck off to wherever you just crawled out under from and just leave me the hell alone." she snarled.

"Please Lillith, I am sorry to bother you, and I wouldn't be here in front of you if I didn't require your assistance, and only you can understand what I need to ask of you. Please just give me five minutes of your time that's all I ask, then I will leave you be, you will never see me again."

"Go on." Lilly said slowly with a continued growl.

"Thank you, you see there is a…firstly let me ask you, have you by any chance seen the news lately, or read about it in the newspapers? You might have possibly noticed an article about people going missing on the west coast."

"I might have," Lilly's eyes seemed to bore into his, "get to the point."

"You see, I was double crossed in Naples by a Mr Venator."

"By Mr who?"

"I see, did you by any chance notice a man rush in surrounded by bodyguards, fall over, grab something, then leave at speed? Well, that bastard snake is Mr Venator."

Lilly drifted into deep thought, her mind juggling through all the horror of that day.

"Yes, strangely enough I do remember him, now get to the point, you're beginning to bore me."

"Well, he fooled me into believing he was a trophy hunter, but he wasn't, he wanted the blood of a vampire."

"What? Whatever for? That blood is just death."

"Maybe so Lillith, but I have discovered he wanted it for a dying multibillionaire known as the Vip, who was well aware that the risk of taking the blood was death, as only a rare few can survive, but he was dying anyway so he took the insane chance."

Lilly was shocked and knew where Carlos was going with all of this, and that's when her interest was piqued.

"Are you telling me…"

"Yes Lillith, the vampire we need to hunt is not your father."

"Hey, wait, wait, wait, what do you mean we?"

"This vampire is an extremely dangerous and cunning one, who needs to be destroyed, we may even need your father's assistance," Carlos spoke urgently to Lilly in hushed tones as to not gain any interest from the other diners nearby in the restaurant, "it was because of Mr Venator that I have lost my hand, it was all down to him that placed you in that nightmare, it was him that upended your world and everything you thought was the truth. He was the bastard that ordered the job, he was after the blood of a vampire to give to the dying Vip for eternal life. Now the Vip has lost control, the bloodlust has overtaken him. He must be destroyed Lilith, do you understand."

Lilly spat out her coffee, turned and gave Carlos her full focus.

"Do you honestly believe in your sad delusional mind that I would ever help you…"

Info regarding Vlad the Impaler, Dracula

·VLAD TEPES A, a 15th Century Prince, who the character of Dracula is inspired by, was supposedly buried near his home in Transylvania, Romania at Lake Snagov.
·It was believed that the corpse of Vlad Tepes 111 Dracula was buried in the Monastery of Snagov island, near Bucharest. But the grave in question does not contain mortal remains, only ox bones and other artifacts were found when it was excavated. So, the mystery remains unresolved there, but other information has come to light.
·He was born between 1431 and 1436 in Sighisoara according to legend and died in 1476 or 1477 so was roughly forty to forty-five years old. The story goes that he was ambushed by an Ottoman patrol and was

reportedly decapitated, and his head sent to the sultan Mehmet 11 in Constantinople.

·Also known for his cruelty which included torturing and impaling his enemies on stakes. This barbarity earned him the gruesome nickname of Vlad the Impaler.

·Archaeological evidence has confirmed a sensational discovery in a crypt within the cloister of the Santa maria la Nova, a 13th century church in Naples. During an excavation conducted by a team of archaeologists, evidence emerged of the presence of a tomb that could belong to Dracula, the legendary vampire.

·Information gathered by the numerous researchers show that from the analysis of Italian manuscripts from the fifteenth and sixteenth centuries, it is possible to hypothesize that Maria Balsa could be the secret daughter of Vlad Tepes who escaped as a child to the persecution of the Turks and was living in Naples in exile, her name was changed to keep her safe. And it was she that had her father's remains buried in the Santa Maria la Nova.

·Researchers believe that Dracula is buried at the cloisters of the church called Santa maria di Nova in Naples, and close to where the event of this story takes place. Dracula means 'son of a dragon'

Is Drago the so-called Dracula, you decide.

BLURB

Dracula never died, for the horrors of his past legacy still exist. He simply embraced the modern world, even changed his name to Drago, living amongst the population of Naples…in plain sight.

Lilly is what might be seen as an average New Yorker, living her life, enjoying her job, with a passion for the arts…or so you might think as a terrifying truth is cruelly revealed to her.

On what she thought was a romantic trip to Naples, Italy, her life is soon turned upside down, becoming a virtual nightmare where many would not survive. Adding to her horror, Lilly discovers that not only is she what is known as a Dhampir, half vampire half human, but her father is the most famous of them all, Dracula himself. She quickly learns that evil does exist and is everywhere, making her question everything she had ever dearly valued, and is soon forced to fight for her very survival. But in doing so, will she choose between remaining human or becoming like him, a blood sucking vampire.

Printed in Great Britain
by Amazon